# Ghosts of Christmas Past

## *A Maddie Brooke Mystery*

Nancy M. Wade

Published in the United States

GARNAN Enterprises, LLC of Ohio.

Copyright 2025 by Nancy M. Wade

All Rights Reserved.

ISBN: 979-8991930185

ISBN: E-979-8991930192

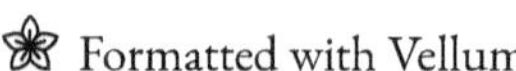 Formatted with Vellum

# Also By Nancy M. Wade

**A Maddie Brooke Mystery**

- Innvitation to Murder
- Mysteries Beneath the Inn
- Death Beneath the Blossoms
- Ghosts of Christmas Past

**A Meadowood Mystery**

- Scarecrows and Corpses
- Deadly Bones
- Reunion With Death
- Deathly Wedding Woes
- Berry Little Murder
- Deadly Secrets
- Merlot Murder
- Subscription to Murder

# Cast of Characters

- **Polly (nee Stewart) Brooke** – Grannie, resident ghost, married Charles Brooke with Southern roots dating back before the Civil War.
- **Madison Leigh Brooke (Maddie)**- 24 year-old granddaughter of Polly, graduate of UVA in Charlottesville, a history major with a nose for research and investigation.
- **Thomas Borden** – long-time employee of the Magnolia Blossom B&B; he is chef and handyman at the inn.
- **Detective Allen Crawford** – a Philadelphia Yankee in the Charlottesville police force; Maddie hopes to tame the Yankee's heart
- **Lionel Hogan** – Maddie's school friend. Lionel is a wiz with computers; works as an I.T. forensic security analyst.
- **Dr. Lily Chung** – Maddie's former roommate at UVA, Lily is Clarkstown's resident physician

- **Detective Lucas Wampler** - Allen's junior partner and love interest of Lily
- **Sally Rawlins** - live-in housekeeper at the inn.
- **Captain David James Brooke** - Maddie's father
- **Guest: Claire Jennings** - single gal looking for her birth mother in region
- **Guest: Evan & Tara McConnell** - young couple expecting their first child, enroute to family visit in PA.
- **Prissy** - the black and white tuxedo cat
- **Luke** – Grannie's protective German shepherd
- **Folks of Clarkstown**

# Ghosts of Christmas Past

*A Maddie Brooke Mystery*

Nancy M. Wade

# Contents

# Chapter One

## Holiday Anticipation

Christmas is coming! No matter how old I get, preparing for Christmas always turns me into a little girl. Decorating the house, baking cookies, wrapping gifts ... I love it all. Thinking of the private holiday party I was planning for Magnolia Blossom Inn put a smile on my face and a spring in my step as I hurried from store to store in Clarkstown.

Three days before Christmas, Clarkstown's historic Main Street sparkled like something out of a holiday snow globe. Garlands of cedar and red velvet bows framed every window. The old-fashioned lampposts wore knitted scarves and felt fabric jolly snowman faces, courtesy of Amanda Fitzwilliams and the Ladies Quilting Circle. Shop windows glowed with miniature villages, toy trains, and twinkling lights. Clarkstown had donned its holiday finery.

"Hello Maddie," called out Joe Wiley, owner of Wiley's Hardware, as I entered the store. Joe occupied his usual place behind the wide front counter, a half-finished crossword puzzle spread out before him.

Handmade aromatic cinnamon brooms rested in a basket along

with scented pinecones near the store's entrance. A large open barrel held bundles of kindling. The scent of freshly cut pine boughs and wreaths hung in the air. Wiley's Hardware prided itself on being a one-stop shop for the do-it-yourselfer, or professional home repairer. Plumbing and electrical supplies, a variety of hand tools, plus every type of hardware fasteners filled the organized shop. Today, I breathed in the fragrance of the holiday greenery that Joe had added, plus I noticed a selection of colorful Christmas lights in his inventory.

"Hi Joe. I'm looking for a pair of solar-powered lanterns I can use on the inn's front porch. Have any left? I saw some the last time I was in, but didn't think to pick them up. Now, I'd really love to have a set to include within my holiday garlands," I answered him.

"Well now, let's just mosey on back here and have a look. I recall seeing some black coach lanterns on a lower shelf."

"Great."

"Hmm, let's see if these are what you had in mind," Joe said as he pulled out a box and opened the flap.

He lifted a twelve-inch tall black lantern with crackle glass inserts and a rectangular solar panel set into the top. Joe flipped over the lantern and revealed a slot holding a double-A battery that gets energized by the solar cell to power the candle-shaped light bulb.

"That's exactly what I was looking for. Do you have a second one?" I asked.

"Yep. Need to get down on these old knees to reach it, but it should be behind that other carton."

Joe pushed aside another box then, kneeling on the concrete floor, he half-crawled into the shelving unit to slide out a second box containing a matching lantern.

I clapped my hands and smiled broadly. "These are wonderful! Thank you. Sorry to put y'all to so much trouble."

"No trouble at all, Miss Maddie. I'm glad to be of service."

"What do I owe you, Joe?"

Joe carried the two cartons back up to the front of the store and keyed a stock number into his register. The new computerized program his son had installed a year ago kept track of inventory and provided an accurate accounting and pricing of the merchandise.

"These lanterns sell for twenty dollars each, but seeing as how it's so close to Christmas and they're not flying off the shelf ... I reckon I can give you a special holiday discount of fifty percent off. How about twenty dollars for the pair?" Joe said with a wink.

"Oh my goodness! You're too kind. Thank you so much," I said as I handed over my money.

Joe tucked the lanterns into a large paper shopping bag.

"Y'all have a merry Christmas. Give my best to Tom," he said.

I pressed an impetuous kiss on his whiskered cheek. "Y'all do the same, Joe. Merry Christmas to you and your family."

He nodded and grinned from ear to ear.

Skipping out of the shop and down the street toward my battered pickup truck, I reveled again in the joy of living in this wonderful small town where neighbors cared for neighbors.

I tucked the shopping bag into the truck cab, then drove over to the Piggly-Wiggly to finish buying a few last-minute food items on my list. Brrr, the weather nipped at my nose as I walked across the grocer's parking lot.

I paused beside the sidewalk chalkboard where little Oliver Perkins, the manager's son, had drawn a snowman in a chef's hat and labeled it: "Today's Special—Cider Brined Turkey!"

Across the street, the Clarkstown Baptist Church carolers gathered in front of the bakery, harmonizing their way through *"Angels We Have Heard on High"* while the scent of warm cinnamon buns floated out through the door. My hungry stomach growled at the delicious smell wafting through the air, reminding me it had been hours since breakfast. Maybe if I hurried, I could finish my food shopping and have time for a quick mug of hot chocolate and one of those sweet sticky buns.

Pushing the cart down the aisles, I mentally ticked things off my list as I added two boxes of Ritz crackers, a can of salted peanuts, and two cheddar cheese balls I wanted for Christmas Eve snacks. Little Smokie cocktail wieners looked appetizing as I tossed them into my cart. I realized that my hunger prompted my additional food purchases; everything looked tasty. No matter. These wieners won't go to waste.

*Hmm, what else?* I dashed into the produce department and picked up a head of lettuce, tomatoes, sprigs of rosemary, fresh thyme, whole cranberries, and two gleaming pomegranates.

*"Tom's going to make magic with this,"* I thought as I completed my shopping.

Tom Borden worked as Magnolia Blossom Inn's chef extraordinaire as well as its handyman and had assumed the role of my surrogate brother. I couldn't run the bed-and- breakfast without him.

Magnolia Blossom Inn existed in a converted pre-Civil War era southern farmhouse with a wide wrap-around porch. The Brooke family had built and lived in the house since 1830, passing it down from one generation to another. I grew up in the old house and on the farm with its cherry and apple orchards. When my mother died, I was only seven years old. My father, a sea captain, brought me to live on the farm with his parents: Charles and Polly Brooke. My father preferred life at sea to raising a lone daughter, so the task fell to my loving grandparents. Every so often, he'd stop by to visit. The last time I had seen my father was at Grannie's funeral. Perhaps this Christmas, he'd make it home. I could only hope.

The inn provided a comfortable living for me with guest reservations and party rentals in our newly renovated barn venue. We've hosted everything from weddings to baby showers to veteran reunions in the barn.

Within an easy commute to the city of Charlottesville, the inn was an ideal location for tourists wanting a quiet spot to stay but close enough to nearby historical attractions like Monticello. Magnolia Blossom Inn offered five bedrooms with private baths for guests and two bedrooms on the third floor with a shared bath for my housekeeper, Sally Rawlins, and me. The large comfortable living room with a brick hearth and fireplace opened into a formal dining room where guests enjoyed a daily sumptuous breakfast prepared by Tom.

We had been booked solid throughout the autumn months, but now that it was close to Christmas, my bookings had dropped off to just a single traveler or two making their way home for the holidays. January was expected to be a slow month with winter weather keeping people at home, yet I looked forward to the time off to putter around the house, catch up on paperwork, and simply relax.

Checking the time on my watch, I decided I could treat myself to that hot chocolate. I zipped up my parka and wrapped my wool scarf tighter as I pushed the cart out of the market and loaded my bags into the truck. Returning the empty buggy to the store, I hurried across the street toward the bakery and those delicious smells.

"Maddie!" came a voice from behind a display stand of poinsettias, causing me to stop with one hand reaching for the bakery doorknob.

I turned to see elderly Amanda Fitzwilliams, my Grannie's dearest friend, bundled in a vintage green plaid cloak, tugging a small cart of groceries down the walk.

"You look like Christmas come to life," I greeted her cheerfully.

Amanda gave a sly wink. "So do you, dear. Though don't let the merry carols distract you. Christmas is coming but so is trouble. I feel it in my bones ... a bad storm's coming. Worse than last year's. I worry about you ... out on that farm all alone. You'd best stock the inn before everyone's snowed in with nothing but cookies and gossip to munch on."

"Oh, the gossip will outlive the cookies," I teased, offering Amanda a steadying hand. "Besides, I'm not alone; I've got Tom and Sally at the inn."

We moved closer to the bakery entrance. I looked longingly at the baked goods on the other side of the glass.

"I'm serious," Amanda said, tapping her gloved fingers to her temple. "My old arthritis acts up when cold damp weather flares up and I feel a storm brewing. The air's gone heavy. The birds are flying low. Nature always knows before the radar does."

"Well, I've got enough provisions to feed an army. Although, I appreciate the warning. I know you're usually right. I've only two guest rooms booked, the rest will be filled with the usual suspects—Lily, Lionel, and of course, Allen and Lucas for a holiday celebration. I'm planning a cozy but lively party filled with holiday cheer."

Behind them, the tinkling of bells announced the door opening on Gerber's General Store, and out bustled Mildred Ginther, wrapped in a fur coat and eavesdropping on our conversation.

Amanda rolled her eyes and mumbled, "Oh dear."

"Did someone say gossip?" Mildred croaked with glee. "Because I just passed the post office, and a young woman was asking for directions to the town records. Asked about the Magnolia Blossom Inn too. Had a fancy suitcase and big city boots. Not from around here."

Amanda snorted. "Mildred, not every stranger's a scandal. Don't go starting trouble where none exists."

"She said her name was Claire Jennings," Mildred added, feigning innocence. "That ring any bells, Maddie?"

I blinked. "Claire? She's one of my booked guests. She told me over the phone she was hoping for a quiet Christmas in the country. Just passing through Virginia. I haven't met her yet."

"Quiet, my foot," Mildred said, eyeing me with sly curiosity.

"She's got that look. Like she's here for more than cocoa and cookies. She's been asking questions all around town. I heard her." Mildred nodded her head as if to indicate that was the final word. She, and she alone, knew what was happening in their small town.

"Maybe she's just alone for the holidays and wants the companionship a small town like Clarkstown can provide," I said, not wanting to give the old biddy any more fodder for gossip. I turned my back on the pair.

Mildred chatted with Amanda about the Baptist church service and who had the best fudge recipe while I waited politely to say goodbye, half listening to the carolers still singing.

Just across the street, Margaret Powers froze when she and her husband stepped out of the pharmacy as Mildred's loud words carried in the crisp air. She dropped her shopping bag, scattering tissues and a box of cough drops onto the sidewalk.

Margaret's face had gone bone white.

Marlon Powers bent stiffly to pick up the spilled items. "What's wrong with you now?" he growled under his breath.

Margaret's lips barely moved. "That old gossip Mildred Ginther, stirring up trouble."

Marlon stood, eyes narrowing. "You recognize who she's talking about?"

"I ... the name sounded familiar, someone I knew long ago." She tugged her coat closed. "It's probably nothing."

But Marlon didn't look away. He studied her face like a man reading an old, dangerous map.

And in that moment, the suspicion that had haunted him for nearly twenty years flared to life again.

"You lied to me," he said quietly, cruelly. "You said you got rid of it. But she's here now. Isn't she?"

Margaret's lips trembled. "No, you're wrong. I don't want to discuss it. Please, not here. Not now ..."

Marlon's eyes darkened. "I'll take care of it."

He dropped the bag into her arms and turned down the alley behind the pharmacy, his boots thumping ominously.

Margaret stood frozen, her breath catching in the cold, unaware that delicate snowflakes fell, clinging to her hair and clothes, promising a white Christmas across the land. How could she explain to her husband the feelings a mother had toward a new life growing within her? She didn't end the pregnancy so many years ago. She couldn't bring herself to do it. Margaret had to give her daughter a chance at life, even if it wasn't with her. Knowing the baby lived and was loved by a good family; that's what kept Margaret going over the past years. She'd kept track of her daughter and her adoptive family but always from afar. Frowning, worry consumed her mind. What was the girl doing in Clarkstown? Did she suspect her birth mother lived here? What would happen if Marlon found the girl? Maybe she better warn Claire. She moved off, her mind set.

I laughed with Amanda Fitzwilliams and dodged Mildred's relentless theories. Little did I know the tragic end of a shameful secret would eventually involve the Magnolia Blossom Inn.

And the storm Amanda warned about?

It had begun.

# Chapter Two

## Jingle Bells

"Good gracious! I ran into Amanda Fitzwilliams and Mildred Ginther in town and I didn't think I'd ever get away. Have our guests arrived yet? I was hoping to beat them home," I told Tom as I carried in the bags of groceries. "I'm totally famished too. I declare, those ladies can talk your ears off."

"Well sit yourself down and try a bowl of this clam chowder I've got simmering. New recipe ... I planned on serving it tonight," Tom said. He spooned the chowder into a small bowl and placed it on the farmhouse table.

Shucking my boots, scarf, and coat, I hung them on the hook in the mud room then slid into a seat at the table. I breathed in the tantalizing aroma rising from the steamy soup. Swallowing a spoonful of the hot chowder, the flavors lingered on my tongue, enticing my palate for more.

"Mmm, this is fabulous." I took several more spoonfuls before continuing. "You know, it started snowing as I left town. At first it just looked like pretty snowflakes, but now it seems to be coming down harder. Do you think we'll get any accumulation?"

"I haven't heard an update on the forecast. I've been busy in here," Tom said as he finished putting away the food items I had bought.

Prissy, the black and white tuxedo cat, curled into a ball under the big farmhouse table. I could hear her loud purring under my feet. Her kitten, Mickey, scampered underfoot chasing a ball of yarn. I had brought Prissy inside when temperatures dropped dangerously, although the cat was no stranger to the cold and preferred living outdoors or in the barn. But she was getting up in years now and no longer had to herd a brood of kittens. After finding homes for her last litter of kittens in September, I kept one male kitty to keep her company and took her to the vet for spaying. She seemed content with this change in her life.

Luke stretched out near the warm heater vent. Mickey jumped on the dog's back and then chased the big tail swishing back and forth on the floor. The large German shepherd raised his head from his outstretched paws and barked in alert.

*"We're in for a doozy of a storm,"* Grannie's voice commented as her ethereal image hovered in front of the window. The snowflakes swirling outside were visible through her translucent body.

"What makes you think so, Grannie?" I asked my resident ghost.

*"I can tell. Reminds me of the blizzard we had back in 1981."*

"Afraid that was before my time. Tom, maybe we better make preparations just in case."

*"Y'all better do that. Trouble is in the air."* With that said, Grannie evaporated in a poof of cold air. I shook my head at her abrupt coming and going.

"I'll check on the generator; make sure we have enough fuel for it in case of a power outage. You better place some candles or lanterns in all the rooms too," Tom said.

"Good idea. I better get a move on. Our guests should be here any moment too," I said as I jumped up and placed my empty bowl in the sink then moved to the pantry off the kitchen.

Hurricane lanterns and boxes of candles filled a lower shelf, ready for any emergency. I scooped up a box of the candles and juggled two of the lanterns, then made my way into the dining and living rooms where I deposited the two lanterns.

Sally Rawlins, our housekeeper, came down the stairs carrying an armload of cleaning supplies. Sally was a widow in her early fifties and shy in nature, with salt and pepper pixie-cut hair and a pleasantly round shape. Her husband's death had left her without life insurance or other means to support herself, forcing her to sell her small home. Her only son lived in Oregon, and her only spinster sister resided in Raleigh. Sally, determined to remain independent and not become a burden on her family, readily accepted my offer last year to work for the inn. She shared the third floor with me.

She raised an eyebrow at me, questioning my actions.

"Every room is ready for guests. I just did a final spritz on the bathrooms and a light dusting."

"Great. Thanks Sally. After you put those things away, take these candles and put them in holders in each of the bedrooms. There should be a candlestick on every dresser."

"Okay. But I thought the new generator would provide us with electricity and we didn't have to worry about a power outage," Sally said, worry tinging her voice.

"It will, but just in case, I'd like to be prepared with candles too. Besides, candle light is so Christmasy," I said with a wink.

Sally took off to do my bidding as I turned to greet the young couple stepping onto our wide veranda. Opening the front door, I smiled and waved them inside.

"Hello! Welcome to Magnolia Blossom Inn! I'm your host, Maddie Brooke. You must be Evan and Tara McConnell. Please come in."

"Thank you. This place looks nice and comfy," Evan said as he looked around the interior of the inn.

"We didn't expect this snow, although the snowflakes look pretty. I'm glad we didn't try to drive further tonight, as much as I'd like to be home with my family by Christmas Eve. I confess I'm exhausted from traveling," Tara said.

The heavily pregnant young woman eased herself onto the comfortable living room sofa and held out her hands to the warm fire that Tom had started in the hearth. Her husband filled out the guest register then joined his wife.

"Would you both like a cup of coffee, or perhaps hot chocolate, before going upstairs to your room? Just sit here and relax. My housekeeper will take your bags upstairs," I offered.

"Coffee sounds wonderful," Evan answered for both of them.

"You have a beautiful place. It's a shame we're only staying the one night," Tara said. "I love your Christmas decorations."

Sally and I had spent the last two weeks decorating the house inside and out. Wreaths made of entwined waxy magnolia leaves and boxwood branches, adorned with red satin bows, hung on each of the windows. Garlands of pine boughs draped the porch railings leading to the impressive front door with its own majestic wreath. Inside, fragrant pine and spruce garlands draped the staircase banister, ending in a festive pineapple, the symbol of hospitality, perched on the newel post with cascading gold ribbons. A garland of woven shiny magnolia leaves and green boxwood draped the mantle and provided a backdrop for a delicate porcelain nativity scene. A seven-foot tall Fraser fir tree stood in a place of honor in front of the bay window, waiting to be decorated in its holiday splendor.

"Thank you. I hope you'll feel up to helping with our tree decorations later on. I'm expecting some friends to join us and have a party of it. Now, I'll just be a minute and get those hot drinks for you."

I scurried into the kitchen and prepared a tray with cream and sugar plus two cups of freshly brewed coffee. I added a small plate containing Tom's gingerbread, cut into small squares. Carrying it back to the living room, I set the tray on the coffee table within easy reach for the guests.

"You're very kind. Thank you for the treat. Is that gingerbread?" asked Tara, inhaling deeply.

"Yes it is. Our chef baked a pan of gingerbread this morning. It's one of his holiday specialties. Enjoy a bite while I get your room key and see that your things have been taken care of. Mister and Missus McConnell, y'all be in our "sunflower" room, the first door on your left at the top of the stairs. Just look for the name stenciled on the door."

"Thanks again, and please call me Evan. My wife is Tara."

"Of course. When is your baby due, Tara?" I asked.

"Any time now. That's why we decided to break our long drive and stay overnight before continuing to Lancaster, Pennsylvania where my parents live. It's a long drive from Knoxville. We really should have started out earlier, allowed more days to travel, but Evan couldn't get time off from work."

"Yes, I can well understand why you'd be tired after such a long journey. Please let me know if you need anything. We'll be serving dinner at six and I hope you'll plan on joining us afterwards to trim the tree," I said as I handed Evan the room key.

Tom had carried the luggage up to the sunflower room and had returned to the kitchen when I heard the distinctive growl of Lionel's Lexus pull in behind the house. Lionel Hogan and Dr. Lily Chung stomped their feet on the porch, knocking off the loose snow, then tapped on the back door while turning the doorknob with the other hand. They entered with a gust of cold air, laughing and shaking snowflakes off their hair.

"Hey y'all, I'm glad you made it," I said, hugging my dear friends.

"Lionel picked me up. He doesn't think my Camry will make it in the snow," Lily said with a jab to Lionel's shoulder.

"Girl ... you've been driving that old thing since you started at UVA. It's ancient. Now that you're a country doctor, you best get yourself an SUV with four-wheel drive," Lionel chided her.

"He's right, you know. Folks in Clarkstown need to know their doctor can reach them, no matter what the weather."

"I'll put it on the top of my to do list for the new year. I promise," Lily said as she reached for the coffee pot and helped herself to a mug. "Want one, Lionel?"

"Yeah. Pour me a cup." He shook Tom's hand and then took a deep breath. "Man, something smells awfully good in here. Tom, you're tickling my taste buds with whatever you have baking in that oven," Lionel said.

"That's a pecan pie you smell," Tom answered.

"Mmm, well if it tastes as good as it smells, we're in for a treat."

My two dearest friends sat across from me, joining me for the Christmas holiday. I loved them both. Lily and I had spent four years as roommates in college until graduation, when she went on to medical school and internship and I came to run the inn. Now that Lily was Clarkstown's family physician, I got to see her more frequently, which thrilled me. Today she appeared stunning in a burgundy silk dress. Lily's long, glossy black hair draped beautifully across the shoulders of the stylish holiday dress.

My normally dapper friend Lionel, always dressed well, and his Christmas attire lived up to the occasion. For tonight's festive dinner he wore an emerald green bow tie, dark green slacks, and a snowy white shirt. A plaid sport coat boasting colors of green, red, and white with fine lines of yellow completed the ensemble. The highlands' tartan colors would have made Grannie proud. Still, I held in my laughter since, on first impression, he looked more like a leprechaun than a Christmas elf.

Lionel had improved the inn's website and online reservation system last year; the inn's business had increased considerably with the new social media presence. He was such a wizard when it came to computers. Lionel worked in cyber- security and computer forensics for the Charlottesville African-American Heritage Center.

The three of us have behaved like the *Three Musketeers* throughout college and since. Lily was the serious one. I guess I could be called the inquisitive one, and Lionel, with his dry wit and flair, kept us all amused.

We huddled together at the big farmhouse table, drinking our coffee and laughing over Lily's tale of being called out to doctor a pet pig. I held the pain in my side from laughing so hard. Even Tom snickered as he listened to the doctor's dilemma about finding a pig's heart beat. The laughter was just dying down when Allen Crawford and Lucas Wampler pulled up and then knocked on the back door.

I rushed to greet them and welcomed them to join our holiday merriment.

Allen and Lucas both served the city of Charlottesville as police detectives, but since Clarkstown didn't have any official law enforcement, they did double duty policing our small town when the need arose. Allen hailed from Philadelphia and took it in stride when local folks ribbed him about his Yankee accent. He and I had grown close yet also butted heads trying to solve Grannie's murder two years ago. He had also rescued me on more than one occasion when the inn unknowingly hosted a crime or two.

I admit that my heart had betrayed me and softened toward the handsome Yankee detective with his wavy dark hair, closely trimmed beard and mustache, and those penetrating hazel eyes. He was a sight for sore eyes, and my heart did a pitter-patter as I grabbed his hand in welcome.

Lily and Lucas Wampler had hit it off right away during a blind date I had arranged for them last summer. Lucas was a local guy with a natural Southern accent and a mischievous personality. He became Allen's partner during a murder case involving local veterans. Lucas's easy charm, tawny-colored hair, and sultry green eyes had won over my best friend, who had previously pledged her devotion to medicine alone. He was the perfect foil for Lily's exotic dark beauty and quieter ways. It tickled me that my matchmaking efforts had been so successful with those two. If only my own romance would follow suit and not be on such a rollercoaster.

Today, Lucas wore a playful red and green elf hat and one of those ugly but funny Christmas sweaters. He immediately went to Lily and wrapped her in an embrace, kissing her lips thoroughly upon greeting. His elf bells jingled gaily as he shook his head.

"Happy holidays!" he whispered in her ear.

Allen pretended to be all business as he hung up his coat and entered the cozy kitchen. He shook Tom's hand and then turned to me, finally pressing a kiss on my cheek.

"Thanks for the dinner invitation. Being here, makes Christmas special for me this year. Hey, roads were getting slippery. Are you expecting any more guests?" he asked.

Wrapping him in a hug, I drank in his rugged good looks and inhaled the faint spicy scent of his aftershave. He wore casual tan corduroy slacks, with a cream-colored cable-knit sweater over a plain dress shirt ... perfect for a snowy day in the country. My fingers touched the dark hair brushing the neck of the bulky sweater.

Planting my own kiss on his cheek, I took a step back. Allen smiled at me, a smile that promised more, then winked.

His action made me forget his question.

"What? Oh yeah, just one. I'll try calling her cell phone," I said. I walked into the foyer to the inn's reception desk and searched my records for the gal's number.

Mildred Ginther has mentioned seeing the girl in town. Claire should be here by now. I hope the deepening snow hadn't posed a problem.

# Chapter Three

## Snowy Night

Luke padded over and pressed his cold nose to my hand before giving a soft whine. He trotted to the front door, turned back to look at me as if to say, "come on", then barked and pawed at the door. His actions caused me to open the portal just as a lone young woman made her way up the steps; her head bent downward against the storm. She carried a bulky tote and a small overnight bag.

I opened the door wider and pulled her into the house while blocking a blast of frigid wind as I shoved the door closed.

"Oh my! I didn't think I'd make it here," the girl declared. "I even spotted a car slid off the side of the road, half buried in the snow on my way here. The roads are terrible." She pulled off a knit cap and peeled away her sodden gloves.

"Are you Claire?" I asked as I took her wet things and coat. "I'll hang these in our mud room close to the heater vent where they can dry."

Sally stepped forward and accepted the damp clothing, taking care of the task for me. I nodded to her and mouthed a thank you.

Claire Jennings signed her name in the register, then looked around the cozy living room with its inviting hearth and welcoming fire. Tall, slim, and clearly nervous, Claire's eyes darted around the room as if she were looking for someone.

The McConnells had retreated to their room to rest an hour earlier, and my friends still grouped in the kitchen. I wondered who the jumpy gal expected to find.

"Here's your key, Claire. You'll be comfortable in the "blossom" room ... top of the stairs and first door on the right. We'll be serving dinner at six, and afterwards, you're welcome to join us in an old-fashioned tree trimming," I said.

"All right. Thank you," she said as she followed me up the staircase.

"Here we are. This is one of my favorite rooms. I hope you'll like the soft lavender and creamy white colors. If I can do anything to make your stay more comfortable, please let me know."

"It's lovely, just like the rest of your inn. I like the fact that this place has history; it's been around a long time. Right?" Claire asked as she bounced lightly on the bed, testing the mattress.

"Well, yes. Magnolia Blossom Inn has been a farm since 1830 but it's only been operating as a bed and breakfast for the past sixteen years. Why do you ask?"

"I was, uh, hoping to talk to somebody that's been here a while. Somebody that might remember a particular person."

"Perhaps we can talk later? Maybe I can help you if you give me more specifics. I've got to go downstairs and tend to dinner arrangements. Y'all come on down when you're ready. Okay?"

Claire nodded as I exited her room. Grannie's ghost popped into sight on the landing.

*"That girl has problems. She reminds me of someone but I can't think who,"* Grannie said, then vanished.

I'll worry about it later. Right now, I have other things on my mind.

Outside, a hush blanketed Clarkstown and surrounding areas. The Appalachian foothills surrounding the little town seemed to hold their breath under a stormy December sky. Snow continued to fall.

Inside, the warmth of the inn's old farmhouse walls hummed with life. A fire crackled in the hearth, and laughter rang out from friends gathered around it. Pine-scented candles glowed next to an arrangement of red and white poinsettias on the dining room's antique mahogany sideboard.

In the kitchen, Tom tossed mixed greens, orange slices, and pomegranate seeds with a champagne vinaigrette for a bright citrus and pomegranate salad. The radio played "Silver Bells." Lily sat at the big table, calmly sipping tea and scrolling through lab results on her tablet. Lionel leaned against the counter beside Tom, pretending not to sneak cookies off the arranged tray.

The phone rang, sounding strident against the melodic "Silver Bells" playing on the radio. Tom reached for the receiver when he saw me carrying an armload of dishes and heading toward the dining room.

"I've got it." He answered the phone and listened to the caller on the other end. I caught him nodding once before speaking. "Yeah, okay. If I see him, I'll give you a holler."

"Who was that on the phone?" I asked, pushing the swinging door connecting the dining room to the kitchen with my hip.

"Oh, that was Jeb Kelce down the road. Wanted to know if we've seen any sign of his horse, Painter. He's missing. Must have gotten out of his stall when the storm started and run off. I told him I'd keep an eye out for the gelding," Tom said.

"Huh, it's not like Painter to leave a warm barn. Odd."

"Hey, snow's coming down fast," Lionel said, peering out the back window as I entered the kitchen. "The forecast just said six inches by nightfall. Maybe more."

"I told Allen and Lucas to bring in more firewood," Lily added, glancing at the back door. "Those two act like the world's ending just because of a few flakes."

I smirked. "That's because neither of them grew up on a farm where your water pump froze or your cow wandered into the woods every time it snowed."

"True," said Tom, licking a dab of champagne dressing off his finger. "City boys."

The back door banged open just then, ushering in a blast of cold air and a cascade of snowflakes that Luke immediately tried to bite mid-air. Prissy meowed indignantly at the cold draft.

"Wood's stacked," Allen said, stomping off his boots and pulling me into a surprising kiss. "Storm's rolling in fast."

The radio announcer broke into the medley of Christmas tunes. *"Blizzard conditions are making roads slick. Albemarle County officials are closing access past the ridge. Residents are advised to shelter at home."*

"That's it then. We're snowed in," I murmured, glancing at the frosted window.

"Looks like it," Allen replied, eyes narrowing. "Which means everyone that's here is staying here."

"Well, no problem. I've got enough rooms if you guys don't mind doubling up," I said.

"Dinner is about ready. Why don't you and Sally call our guests and have them come down?" Tom suggested as he stirred the enormous pot of clam chowder for our first course.

"What can we do to help, Tom?" asked Lily as she tied an apron around her slim waist.

"How about filling that tea kettle with fresh water and putting it on? I've got coffee brewing. Maybe Lionel can open those two bottles of wine. Maddie's got the table all set and I think Sally has called in the guests, so we should be ready," Tom said.

"Okay. Everything looks delicious," Lily replied.

Evan and Tara McConnell strolled into the dining room. Dinner plates edged in a tiny holly and berry pattern sat atop shiny green or red chargers, adding to the festive theme. Candles glowed at both ends of the table, flanking a fragrant centerpiece of greenery, tiny silver bells, and red carnations. Sparkling crystal stemware and silverware reflected the soft light.

"Oh my! The table is lovely," Tara exclaimed.

"Thank you. It's a rare occasion when our inn guests join us for the evening meal so I wanted to make it special. Please sit wherever you like," I said with a wave of my hand as I turned and spotted Claire standing timidly in the doorway.

"Come in, Sweetie," gestured Sally, recognizing a shared shyness with the girl. "Take a chair."

Claire nodded, glanced at the young couple, then sat across the table from them. Lily came into the room and placed a basket of fluffy, buttery dinner rolls on the table. She smiled and acknowledged the guests.

Lucas joined us. Lily patted the chair next to her for Lucas, and he immediately took her up on it, never one to pass up a chance to be near her. I loved watching them; they were such a romantic pair. Sighing, I admitted I envied their openness and carefree affection.

Allen and Lionel entered, holding two bottles of wine. They made the rounds, filling wine glasses. I noticed Sally slipped in next to Claire.

"Well, I hadn't planned on a snowy white Christmas, but I'm thrilled to have everyone here tonight. Thank you for choosing to spend part of your Christmas celebration with us. Guess I better make some introductions. I'll start on the left side of the table. Claire Jennings is sharing her Christmas with us. Next to her is my best friend Doctor Lily Chung and her beau, Lucas Wampler. You all know Sally Rawlins. Sally resides at the inn. I don't know what I'd do without Sally or Tom. You'll meet our wonderful chef, Tom Borden, in just a minute. He's preparing bowls of hot New England clam chowder for everyone."

At that moment, Tom entered the dining room with a large tray filled with steaming bowls of chowder. He went around the table, serving each person, receiving oohs and aahs from the seated guests.

"Hope no one has a seafood allergy. Our feast tonight favors an East coast menu in honor of our guests: the McConnells, who hail from Pennsylvania, and our resident Yankee, Detective Crawford, who used to call Philadelphia home," Tom said with a flourish.

Claire cast a stricken stare at Allen when Tom announced he was a detective. I caught her sudden intake of breath and the frightened look that entered her eyes before she quickly lowered her head and focused on the plate before her.

Standing, I waved my hand toward the right side of the table to finish my introductions.

"Okay, before your soup gets cold, let's bid welcome to Tara and Evan McConnell who drove up from Knoxville enroute to Pennsylvania." Everyone nodded or smiled. "This is my dear friend Lionel Hogan, and Allen Crawford is next to me," I said as I took my seat at the head of the table.

Spoons dipped into the rich broth as everyone concentrated on the creamy chowder. Outside, the wind rattled windowpanes as the snowstorm raged. A boom of thunder shook the house, causing both Tara and me to jump.

"Oh my goodness! I didn't know it could thunder during a snow storm," Tara said. Her husband squeezed her hand for comfort.

"We're okay folks. That's called thundersnow. It's rare, but in severe storms like this, we can experience both thunder and lightning. This old house has stood for almost two hundred years and weathered more storms than this," Tom said in a level voice.

Tara took a deep breath. "Sorry. I don't mean to be so skittish."

"Don't you worry about it," Lily spoke up. "You're pregnant. Those raging hormones cause your emotions to shift into high gear. That loud thunder startled me too. By the way, Tara, if you need anything or don't feel well, just let me know. I'm here for you."

Tara smiled and shot Lily a grateful look. "I must say, this inn thinks of everything, even a physician on call for pregnant guests." We all chuckled, and the mood lightened.

Sally jumped up and began clearing the soup bowls as Tom went back to the kitchen to plate our main entrees.

"Tom told you we were having a New England supper tonight. He's cooked creamy roasted garlic mashed potatoes, sauteed green beans almondine plus crispy fried oysters as the main dish. In keeping with the holiday season, I think you'll enjoy his citrus and pomegranate salad too. But to inject a bit of our southern taste to the dinner, Tom made a sweet corn spoonbread. It's similar to a soft cornbread pudding. Y'all need to try it," I said as Tom and Sally carried in the individual plates of food.

"Eat up folks but save some room for dessert. I've got a cranberry-orange cheesecake or a gingerbread trifle," Tom announced as we all savored the wonderful food.

Claire and Tara both clapped their hands at the dessert announcement, and even Allen, normally so solemn, wore a grin that stretched from ear to ear.

Fully sated and stifling yawns, everyone collapsed onto chairs or sunk into soft sofa cushions in front of the crackling fire. Lily insisted Tara sit in the Queen Anne side chair and elevate her feet on a small footstool. Soft Christmas carols played in the background under murmurs of conversation.

Sally dragged out two large cartons of Christmas decorations and opened them near the tree. Cups of coffee plus a teapot of steeped black tea, spiced with cinnamon and cloves, sat on a tray for the weary guests. A second tray held a choice of mulled cider or more goblets of wine.

"When I was a child, my grandparents made decorating the Christmas tree a special celebration and tradition of the holiday. Tonight, I'd like to share that tradition with all of you and ask you to help decorate our story tree," I said.

"Why do you call it a story tree?" asked Tara. She sipped a cup of the blended holiday tea and relaxed against the cushions.

"It's a story tree because every ornament tells a story ... a memory of a vacation trip, a birthday, or a special event in my life. Whenever we traveled, we bought an ornament to remind us of the trip. I've got ornaments from almost all fifty states plus some from state parks or historic locations."

"I love that idea," Tara said and clasped Evan's hand. "We need to start that tradition with the baby."

Claire pulled a silver disk from the carton. Engraved on the disk was the five-ring symbol of the Olympics. She held it up for all to see.

"That one is from the winter Olympics of 2002 held in Salt Lake City. I was only a baby and didn't live here then, but Grannie and Grandpa Charles went to it. Grannie loved the ice skating competitions. Go ahead and hang it on the tree," I said.

Allen took the next ornament, a faded tin soldier, and gave a low whistle. "This thing's older than me."

He handed the ornament for me to see.

"Grandpa carried it during his time in the military and during the Vietnam War," I said, passing it carefully back to him. "Hung it on every Christmas tree no matter where he was stationed."

Grannie's ghost shimmered in the candlelight. She smiled as she watched the decorating. Tears glistened in her eyes.

*"Thank you for keeping the tradition alive,"* Grannie said.

Lily and Lionel exchanged a silent communication with me, touched by Grannie's words. They were among the few people who could see and hear my grandmother's ghost.

Lily hung a delicate glass angel on a branch. "This one is beautiful."

"That was my mother's," I told her. "She bought it at a street market in Paris. I remember she said it made rainbows when the lights hit the crystal prisms."

I hung the next ornament. A navy blue and orange-colored glass ball with the UVA insignia on it. My alma mater.

Even Sally, our no-nonsense housekeeper, softened when she pulled out a star made of yellowed construction paper. Covered in glitter, with the dried paste falling off in spots. "Your Grannie let me make this when I was twelve," she said. "My Ma and Pa had left me with your Grannie when they drove to a funeral out of state. Didn't have much, but she made me feel like family here. I can't believe she kept it."

"I didn't know that. So you recall being at Magnolia Blossom when you were a child too. You never told me that story."

Sally sniffled and tucked the star into the evergreen branches.

Tara picked up the next ornament from the carton. She held the tiny carved rocking-horse in the palm of her left hand. Frowning, she stared at the wooden ornament. She suddenly pressed her palm against her forehead and closed her eyes. Lily rushed to her side, fearing the pregnant woman was about to swoon.

"Are you all right?" Lily asked.

Tara whispered, "I sense a sadness in the object. I, uh, felt an overwhelming grief holding the horse."

"Hmm, I read once about expectant mothers becoming more sensitive to spiritual energy, but I've never witnessed it before this. Maddie, what's the story on this rocking horse?" Lily asked and held up the ornament.

"I don't know really. It probably was Grannie's decoration from when she was a child."

Tara hung it on a lower branch of the tree and then sat down, quietly studying the flames dancing within the hearth.

The mood in the room became somber until Lionel found a colorful blown-glass clown ornament within the box and proudly hung it on the tree. He made up an outrageous story about the history of the clown and how it ran away from a circus. Leave it to Lionel to restore everyone's gaiety.

We laughed and exchanged stories of our childhood memories of Santa Claus, Christmas trees, and favorite gifts as we worked. At last, the decorated tree stood in all its glory. Tiny white lights twinkled among the myriad of ornaments: some glass, metal, wooden, or glittery paper. Gathering near the tree, we sang an impromptu chorus of "O Tannenbaum", clasping hands and swaying to the tune.

Cookies were nibbled and drinks drunk. Guests yawned. It was time to call it a night.

Evan helped Tara rise. With her hand resting on her protruding belly, she turned to bid us all goodnight and mentioned their plan to leave in the morning for her parents' house.

Allen shook his head. "Not happening. Roads are drifted over. Sorry, you're here until the plows come through."

Tara teared up and cried softly. "Oh dear! I wanted to be with my family for Christmas, especially with the baby coming. Now we're snowbound."

"I'm sorry. Maybe by later tomorrow we'll get plowed out," I said.

"A neighbor on the next farm over has a plow on his tractor. He usually takes care of us."

As the couple started up the stairs, a clap of thunder boomed and a loud crack of lightning split the night sky. It struck close by. You could smell ozone in the air.

Tara screamed.

Allen and Lucas ran toward the back door. Tom had already thrust his feet into snow boots and shrugged on a coat. The men grabbed flashlights and then headed out into the night to check for damage.

I stood at the door, watching them through the frosty window.

*I don't like it. Something's wrong,* Grannie whispered.

Luke barked and pawed at the door. The hackles on the ruff of his neck rose; a low growl rumbled in his throat.

Within minutes, the men tramped back onto the porch. Knocking wet snow off their boots, they hurried back into the house and left shoes and coats to dry in the mud room.

"Looks like the lightning struck that old elm tree near the barn. Split it in half, right down the middle of the trunk," Tom said.

"Strangest thing I ever saw," commented Lucas. "You could see the wood scorched black."

"I checked for signs of any burning embers. Didn't see any. I think it's safe; it shouldn't flare up," Allen said.

"Okay. Guess we better all go to bed. Allen and Lucas can use the "ivy" room at the end of the hall. Lionel, you bunk with Tom in the "daisy" room and Lily can have the pink "meadow flower" room. Sally and I will be in our rooms on the third floor if anyone needs us."

"Good. Glad I don't have to sleep in that frilly pink bed with the canopy again," Allen muttered as the others climbed the stairs. He gave me a look and inclined his head toward the living room. Catching his message, I nodded with a smile.

Christmas tree lights twinkled. The cozy room was lit only by the glow of the fire in the hearth. Allen poured us each a glass of wine. I kicked off my shoes and curled my legs under me as we snuggled together on the sofa, watching the embers dance and float up the chimney.

"Mmm, this is nice," I whispered.

Allen held me in the circle of his arms. "This is how the holidays should be spent ... just the two of us, a glass of wine, and a toasty fire on a cold snowy night."

"Sounds like a Hallmark movie," I said with a chuckle. "But you better amend your math," I said as I pointed to Luke stretching out in front of the hearth and Prissy, who had curled up on the other end of the sofa.

Allen laughed as he acknowledged the pets. Holding up his glass, he toasted, "To us and a very merry Christmas."

The fire crackled; Prissy purred. We cuddled, enjoying the solitude as the clock ticked another hour gone by.

"As much as I'd love to stay, I'd better get to bed. Morning comes early with guests in the house. I've got to help Tom with breakfast chores," I said as I rose and stretched my arms above my head.

"Okay."

We checked all the door locks and banked the fire, then turned in for the night.

Outside, the wind howled louder, cutting off the world.

Inside, the Magnolia Blossom Inn was about to give up its secrets —whether the living or the dead wanted them revealed.


It was after midnight when Luke woke me with his low growls from the foot of the bed. I sat up, throwing off my covers. Searching for Grannie, my heart thudded until I spotted her. Grannie's ghost shimmered into sight. Her hair was piled in a high holiday bun, and she wore the old tartan shawl she always brought out at Christmastime.

*"There's something else in this house tonight,"* Grannie whispered.

"What do you mean?"

*"Another spirit. Older than me. Angry. It's been awakened, released from the split tree. It's downstairs."*

Luke growled again and then bolted for the hallway door, barking sharply.

"Hush Luke. You'll wake up the entire house."

I threw on a robe and followed him downstairs, heart pounding. Moonlight bathed the parlor, and the fire was still low in the hearth.

Allen silently walked up behind me, his bare feet making no sound on the wooden floor. I nearly jumped out of my skin as his hand touched my shoulder.

"What is it? I heard Luke growl."

All I could do was point.

Someone ... or something, had written in the condensation on the living room window.

***Revenge is mine.***

# Chapter Four

## Spirits

The aroma of freshly brewed coffee and warm cinnamon rolls drifted through the Magnolia Blossom Inn, mingling with the sharp scent of snow and pine. Sunlight struggled through the thick clouds outside, casting a blue-gray hue over the winter-covered hills. Inside, the kitchen and breakfast nook glowed golden from the fire-light and the sparkle of garlands draped across the windows.

I poured orange juice into a cut-glass pitcher while Tom fussed over scrambled eggs at the stove, humming "Let It Snow."

Allen and Lucas squeezed in next to Lily at the kitchen farm-house table. My friends preferred the informal kitchen setting, allowing the inn's paid guests to occupy the dining room. The men gripped hot mugs of coffee and gobbled down plates of fluffy eggs and crisp bacon.

Lionel, wearing a borrowed flannel shirt that didn't match his plaid pajama pants, had set up his laptop on the corner of the table to check on the latest news. I had to laugh at his attire, a far cry from his normal debonair fashion.

"Storm dumped almost nine inches overnight," he said, clicking through computer screens. "Roads shut down. Electric is off in half the county. But your generator's keeping things cozy. We're officially a holiday hideaway."

"Told you the generator would get us through the storm," Tom said.

"We need to check the barn and grounds for signs of any other damage when we're done here," Allen told Lucas.

Allen shot me a look with a nod, and I knew he was thinking of the midnight message left on the window.

At the dining room table, Evan and Tara sat side by side, hands entwined.

Tara's round belly peeked beneath her chunky red sweater. "This baby's kicking like she's dancing in there," she said with a giggle.

"She's eager for her first Christmas," Evan said, eyes wide with wonder as he looked out at the whitewashed world beyond the window. "Or maybe it's the cinnamon rolls I smell."

I smiled at them both, grateful for their uncomplicated joy. "Tom's cinnamon rolls are famous for waking babies and adults alike. Eat up. Enjoy the eggs. You'll need your strength if we all pitch in to dig out the front paths later."

They chuckled, and for a moment the inn felt like any cozy Christmas card come to life.

"I'm going to go check on Claire," I said, excusing myself and heading upstairs.

I knocked lightly on Claire's bedroom door. Claire opened the door and then went to stand by the window, staring at the frosty scene outside and snow-covered barn. Her hands clutched the windowsill tightly.

"You all right?" I asked gently. Stepping into the room, I noticed a journal laying open on the nightstand; the name Marlon Powers jumped off the page. My eyebrows shot up in recognition. Why would this young girl have that name in her journal?

Claire startled, then forced a smile. "Yes ... just a beautiful view. The snow." She left the window and walked over to the bed, nonchalantly closing the journal from my prying gaze.

"Breakfast is ready. Do you want to come down? Can I do anything for you?"

"I'll be down in a minute. I, um, wanted to ask your help. Maybe you or Tom might remember a woman who lived near here ... oh, I'm not explaining this very well. Guess I just need to say it. I'm searching for my birth mother," Claire said in a shaky voice. She studied my face as if she were expecting a sign of my disapproval or shock.

I could see the stress in her eyes. "I'll try to help you as much as I can, but you need to consider the consequences, Claire, if you find her."

She wrung her hands and nodded. "It's all I can think about."

"Come down for breakfast. We can talk more later. Okay?" I said as I patted her arm, then turned to go.

I returned to the kitchen to help Tom with breakfast when suddenly a piercing scream made us all jump.

Dashing through the dining room door, I ran into the foyer and looked toward the staircase. Luke barked and growled, launching himself onto the top landing.

Claire lay crumpled on the floor at the bottom of the steps, her face pale, and blood oozed from a cut on her head. With one leg twisted beneath her, she threw her arms out to her sides. Claire's eyes fluttered open but then rolled back again.

"Claire!" I knelt beside her just as Lily and Lucas rounded the corner.

"I've got this," Lily said, already reaching for Claire's wrist. Her fingers checked the pulse at the neck, then the wrist again. "She's breathing but weak. Pulse is thready."

"I just left her. She was coming down for breakfast," I said.

"Lucas, please grab my medical bag from my room," Lily commanded as her trained hands checked for other injuries.

Grannie's ghost appeared ... solemn, hovering at the foot of the steps.

*"Careful, Maddie,"* she warned, eyes darted toward the window where the wind swirled snow thick and white. *"That evil spirit is getting closer. And it's not shy."*

I swallowed hard and whispered, "Define 'not shy.'"

*"Mean enough to slam a door in your face or knock you down the stairs,"* she said. *"And if I could get rid of it myself, I would, but I'm not sure I can."*

Lucas carried the injured girl down the hall into my study. A narrow daybed sat against the wall across from my desk and filing cabinets. He laid her down carefully on the bed as Lily rushed to tend the head injury and monitored her vital signs.

"What happened?" asked Allen as he stood in the doorway next to me, watching.

"I don't know. Maybe she tripped? There aren't any rugs at the top of the stairs or on the individual stair treads to prevent this kind of accident. I don't understand it," I said.

"She'll be all right. Head wounds always look worse than they are but she took a bad tumble. I'll sit with her for awhile. She should wake up soon," Lily said as she covered Claire with a heavy crocheted blanket.

Tara and Evan both cast anxious looks at me as I entered the dining room.

"Is Claire okay? Is she badly hurt?" Tara questioned in a soft voice. Her fingers rested protectively on her belly.

"She's in good hands," I reassured her. "Dr. Lily won't let anything happen to her."

"Don't worry honey. It was just an accident. People fall on stairs all the time," Evan said as he tried to reassure his wife.

"But Evan ... what about that strange dream I had? I saw a man push her," Tara whispered.

My eyes widened at her words.

Allen and Lucas bundled up, then went to inspect the property. They started on the front porch and then made their way around to the rear of the house and toward the barn. One door stood open, banging against the siding in the heavy wind. The men stepped inside the barn turned party venue, pulling the heavy door closed and inspected the building. They locked the door behind them when they left.

Next, Allen checked the small garden shed door. It was shut tight and locked. The chickens squawked inside the warm hen house but appeared all right. Maddie or Tom would have to come out and collect the eggs. He didn't want any part of that farm chore.

Lucas and Allen trudged through the deep snow. A drift at least three feet deep had piled up against the main barn entrance. A howling wind still blew loose snow into the air; the ice crystals shimmered, catching the meager glint of sunlight.

Both men stopped and examined deep footprints embedded in the newly fallen snow. Allen pointed to the path taken.

I waited with Tom in the kitchen until Allen returned from checking the perimeter of the property. He took off his gloves and stood behind my chair.

"There were fresh tracks around the barn. Boot prints, looping around the back—someone circling. Not mine, not Lucas's. We also found a horse in your barn, tied inside one of the stalls. I don't think it wandered in there on its own."

Tom and I both exchanged worried glances.

"Was it a black and white horse?" Tom asked.

"Yeah, why?" asked Allen.

"That sounds like old Painter. Belongs to Jeb Kelce down the road. He certainly didn't stroll in during a snow storm and tie himself up," I said.

"Could it be a local neighbor?" Lucas asked. His doubt colored his voice.

"Not in this weather. And not around that barn. I don't like it," Tom said.

"Somebody is here. Why hasn't he come up to the house?" I asked. "Where is he?"

"I don't like it. Maybe we better take turns doing guard duty ... at least keep lookout. I'll take the first shift tonight," Allen said.

"Do you think we might be in danger? You've got me worried," I said.

I glanced between the lawmen, trying to read their expressions. We had a prowler on the property. Either that or the evil tree spirit is capable of leaving footprints behind.

# Chapter Five

## Past Ghosts

Drinking coffee, while a German shepherd paced like a metronome and stared toward the parlor like a specter was about to materialize, only increased my jitters. The caffeine didn't help. *"What does Luke see, that I can't?"*

Taking the big dog by the collar, I led him toward the front door. He needed a romp in the snow, and it wouldn't hurt if he patrolled the grounds.

"Okay, Luke," I murmured, "either it's a squirrel in the Christmas tree or…" I trailed off, not wanting to say "ghost" out loud with guests near. "Out you go."

Grannie's voice floated in from the corner of the room. *"Not me this time, sugar. He feels the other one."*

I glanced toward the hearth. Sure enough, there appeared my grandmother dressed in her favorite cranberry wool skirt and cream cardigan, looking like she'd just stepped out of a 1960s holiday party. But her usual mischievous sparkle was missing.

"You mean the second spirit?" I asked under my breath, hoping Lionel wouldn't overhear from the next room.

*"Yes,"* she said, her tone low. *"It's restless, child. And it's not fond of strangers."*

Claire's soft moan from my office ended our spectral wondering. I carried my coffee with me and found Lily sitting at her bedside, checking her pulse.

"You're awake," I said softly. "How are you feeling?"

Claire blinked, her eyes glassy but focused. "Embarrassed. Confused. I'm sorry for ... whatever happened."

"No apology necessary," Lily said firmly. "You fell on the stairs."

Claire's gaze moved to me. "I was pushed. I felt a hand on my back."

"Are you sure?" I asked and glanced at Lily to read her reaction to Claire's accusation.

"I think so. Oh, I dunno. Maybe it's stress from dodging the truth of my past, plus the holidays. You know I came here to find my mother. She abandoned me as a baby. I need to know why." Tears filled Claire's eyes.

The words hung in the air like frost.

"I'm sorry," I said. "That's... a lot to carry, but why would you think she'd be here?"

"Not here at the inn, but in town. I don't know her full name, just that she lived in Clarkstown around 2001 and was unmarried. My adoptive parents passed away two years ago in a car accident. When I went through their things, I found a note in my file ... *Margaret Q.* That's all. It was my birth mother's name."

"I think I saw you in town the other day, before you arrived at the inn. A friend of mine said she ran into you at the post office and you were asking questions. How did you know to come to Clarkstown if you didn't have a full name?" I asked.

Claire lowered her eyes and pulled the cover up under her chin. "After my mother ... my adoptive mother, died, I went through her things, like I said. A faded envelope, addressed to me, held a birthday card. Inside, it read happy eighth birthday. No signature and there was no return address but the post mark said Clarkstown. My mother never gave it to me; I'm not sure why she even kept it but I thought the town was important and I remembered it."

I tried to keep my face neutral, but my mind was already making connections. "Margaret Q. All right. That's not much to go on, but we've got Lionel to help. He's a wizard."

"Hey, I heard my name. Are you singing my praises again? Do I get a superhero cape?" Lionel called from the doorway, holding his ever-present laptop. "Because I feel like I deserve one."

I laughed at his antics.

"Hey yourself, super-hero. I've got a project for you. But first I've got to get some food into this gal before she faints from hunger." I turned to Lily and Claire as Lionel opened his laptop on my office desk. "Claire, are you strong enough to come into the dining room or kitchen for breakfast?"

Lily nodded and supported Claire as she swung her legs off the narrow bed and waited while Claire's head swam dizzily. She pressed her hand to her forehead and took a deep breath.

"Give it a second. Take your time. Okay, let's try standing," Lily said as she held onto Claire's arm.

Claire cautiously stood and took a tentative step. She looked between Lily and me, then smiled slightly.

"I am kind of hungry. Did I miss much while I was out?"

"Not a thing, except breakfast. I'm sure Tom can scramble you a couple eggs in a flash and saved some cinnamon rolls for you too. How's that sound?" I asked as I helped her walk down the hall and into the dining room.

Sally rushed to greet Claire. She sat with the lonely gal while she ate, offering her a friendship they both needed.

Evan and Tara had retreated to the living room, relaxing before the fire and listening to Christmas music. Tara sat with her hand resting on her belly. I noticed she wore a pensive expression, as if she concentrated solely on the tiny being within her.

An hour later, Lionel and I sat in the small office. Luke stretched out at my feet while Lionel clicked away like a man trying to win a typing contest.

"How many last names could there be that started with the letter Q in Clarkstown? That's not too common," I said.

"Hmm, that's what I thought. I'm checking the census records from 2000. I found three families with a last name starting with Q. Only one family showed a daughter named Margaret. Margaret Quinton," Lionel said.

He pointed to the census report displayed on the screen and ran his finger down the lines where he highlighted the Quinton name.

"Okay. Looks like her age was reported as seventeen when the census was taken. She could be Claire's mother," I said.

Lionel switched websites and opened up county records of births and marriages. He smiled broadly, like the Cheshire cat.

"Got something," he said finally. "Margaret Quinton married Marlon Powers in March of 2002. I don't see any reference to a birth. They live on the east side, big property. Wealthy. He's head of the Powers Lumber Mill. She's on the county historical society board, organizes fundraisers for the library ... basically, Clarkstown royalty."

I chewed my lip. "I know those people. That means if Margaret is Claire's mother, she's been keeping this secret for over twenty years. Doubtful she'd be very happy about Claire coming into town and opening up that can of worms."

Lionel leaned back. "And secrets in small towns? They're like

Christmas fruitcake. Nobody wants them, but somehow they keep showing up."

Before I could respond, Grannie materialized right behind Lionel. Lionel jumped.

"Jeez Grannie, let a guy know when you're going to pop in. You almost gave me a heart attack."

*"Sorry. I keep forgetting you aren't as used to me as Maddie."*

"Grannie, did you know the Quinton family? Do you recall their daughter Margaret?" I asked her.

*"Yes. Snob hill people. Your grandpa couldn't abide them. Margaret was a pretty gal but shy. Seems to me there was talk about her getting in the family way, you know how folks love to gossip. There was a boyfriend her parents didn't approve of ... not sure what happened to him. She went away to stay with her aunt in Atlanta, supposedly to help nurse the woman, and when she came back she married a young soldier. That would be Marlon Powers. He deployed right after the wedding to that horrible war in Iraq ... like Tom did."*

"Okay. So she could have given birth secretly. She may be Claire's best lead," I said.

"What type of people are they? Looks like they're involved in civic events, at least she is," Lionel said.

*"Margaret is still shy but takes her position in society and responsibilities seriously. On the other hand ... her husband Marlon is a spiteful, mean man,"* Grannie said and then disappeared in a poof.

"Do you want me to give this information to Claire? It's public records... the Quinton-Powers marriage. Legally, I don't think we have any right to keep it from her," Lionel said as he printed off the Powers biography page.

"Let me think about it. What if we're mistaken? It would create a scandal for a perfectly innocent woman."

Snowdrifts banked against the Magnolia Blossom Inn so high they kissed the lower panes of several windows. The air held a glassy chill that made your lungs ache when you breathed too deeply, and the quiet, broken only by the occasional groan of snow sliding from the roof, was the kind that makes you strain to listen harder.

Allen and Lucas had insisted on checking the property again, "just in case." I'd bundled up and trailed after them with a basket in hand, planning on collecting eggs from the hen house. The snow swallowed my boots to mid-calf, dampening my pant leg. My cheeks felt like brittle porcelain. As usual, the hens squawked and objected to my stealing their eggs; the difference this time was they couldn't peck me through my heavy gloves. Their roost was warm despite the frigid air outside thanks to the heat lamps installed high above the nests. My utility bill next month will reflect the added expense, but it was better than losing the flock. Once the temperatures returned to normal, we could cut back on the heat.

I hurried to complete my chores and plodded back onto the rear porch. Rubbing my hands together, I watched the men trudge ahead.

I was about to call for them to hurry back inside when Lucas's voice cut through the stillness.

"Allen ... over here."

The tone of the young detective's voice piqued my curiosity. I placed my egg basket inside the mudroom and then hurried to catch up with Allen.

He crouched beside the drift that skirted the east side of the inn. The snow wasn't smooth anymore. A distinct line of footprints ... deep and deliberate, ran parallel to the wall before disappearing around the corner.

I felt the hair at the nape of my neck prickle. "Those aren't from you two."

Allen straightened, scanning the tree line. "Nope. Too close to the house. Whoever it was, came right up here."

"And left without knocking?" I asked. My voice sounded smaller than I wanted it to as my attempted humor fell flat.

"Or without wanting to be seen," Allen muttered.

We followed the tracks, my breath coming out in white bursts. The cold had a strange metallic taste, as if the air itself was made of tin. When we rounded the corner, Allen stopped so abruptly, I almost plowed into him.

"Madison! Stop!" Allen's voice rang out in the still air.

I shook my head and forged ahead, ignoring his order.

The lone elm stood ahead, half its branches blackened and twisted from where lightning had struck during the thundersnow. The scarred trunk split clear down the middle as if Paul Bunyan had taken a giant axe to it. From one thick limb, something hung ... swinging slightly in the wind at the end of a rope.

It took a moment for my eyes to focus. And then I wished they hadn't.

"Maddie, please, stay back. No one should have to see this," Allen said as he tried to shield me.

I couldn't help it and looked again at the blackened tree.

A man's body. Dangling. The rope creaked as it shifted, rubbing against the hard tree bark, the sound a cold counterpoint to the hammering of my pulse.

Lucas swore softly. "Who is that?"

# Chapter Six

## Speculation

Allen moved closer, crunching through the snow. I stood rooted to the spot in the deep snow, staring at the macabre figure swinging in the icy wind. Lucas waited with me.

When Allen came back, his face was pale, his jaw tight. "Marlon Powers."

"Are you sure?" I asked. My breath froze into a crystal fog as I spoke.

"Yeah, I'm pretty sure. Powers and his wife are prominent citizens around here and carry some clout. Even a Yankee like me knows who pulls the strings of local politics. My boss, Chief Barlow, will not like this."

"What's Marlon Powers doing at Magnolia Blossom?" I asked in a whisper. My mind flew to the conversation I'd had with Claire.

When we got back inside, the warmth of the parlor felt almost wrong after what I'd just seen. I needed to attend to my guests. A fire crackled in the hearth, making the room feel warm, toasty, and inviting; however, only one person occupied the room.

Claire had vanished upstairs into her room. No amount of knocking from Sally could coax her out.

Tara McConnell hovered near the hearth, her eyes haunted. "Maddie," she whispered, "I've been having dreams. Premonitions. I keep seeing a gray-haired man, dressed in odd old clothes. He's not friendly. His eyes are cold, mean. He looks at me strangely. I saw him again last night through our window, standing under that blackened tree in the snow."

"It's probably nothing to worry about. Like you said, it's only a dream. You sit down and rest. Would you like to look through these magazines?" I asked her as I placed the Christmas issue of *Southern Living* on the side table.

Tara nodded to me, her expression thoughtful, as I left her and made my way back to the kitchen.

Arranging a platter with the cheese ball and crackers I had bought the other day, I added some fresh grapes, tangerine slices, and a bowl of the little smoked sausages heated in the microwave to make an appetizing charcuterie board.

As I worked, I felt the faint brush of cold air at my shoulder. Without looking, I knew Granny's ghost had appeared. Her voice was tight, almost brittle. *"He's real, Maddie. And he's dangerous. I can't hold him back."*

I swallowed hard. "The lightning must have—"

*"Released him,"* Granny finished, her eyes sweeping the corners of the room as though she could still see him. *"And he's looking for revenge."*

"Who is he, Grannie? How can we fight a specter?"

No answer came.

I carried the platter of snack foods into the living room and placed it in the center of the coffee table. Adding a stack of napkins and small dessert-sized paper plates next to the food, I offered Tara a snack.

"Can I bring you a drink? Hot chocolate or perhaps something cold to drink?" I asked Tara as her husband strolled into the room and joined her.

"Something hot, please," she said.

Lily entered the room and took a chair near Tara. She chatted with the young couple and nibbled on some of the cheese and crackers.

I nodded and then watched Tom as he worked. My eyes scanned the living room; the lights glowed on the Christmas tree, and the battery-operated pillar candles had come on. The house felt different to me after the discovery of the body.

Tom laid a bundle of firewood and kindling near the fireplace, close at hand to keep the fire burning during our Christmas Eve celebration. As he stood, he read my worried expression.

"What's wrong?" he asked.

I inclined my head toward the kitchen, and he nodded, then followed me back to where we could speak privately.

"Allen and Lucas found Marlon Powers' body with a noose around his neck, hanging in the elm tree. Grannie is picking up on strange vibes from an evil ghost that was released by the lightning strike. Other than that, everything is just peachy!"

If it wasn't so horribly alarming, I would have laughed at the shocked look on Tom's face.

"I saw the footprints in the snow earlier. Does Allen suspect Marlon Powers made those prints prowling around the house? Who killed him or was it suicide?" Tom asked.

"Heaven only knows. Who else is here except all of us? I can't imagine Claire killed him or even had the strength to lift a heavy man, especially with her recent concussion. Definitely Tara McConnell didn't do it unless being nine months pregnant gives you super powers." I snorted and glanced toward Lionel and the detectives grouped around the laptop. "Surely none of us are guilty?"

"Hmm, well, who does that leave?" Tom asked as he pulled out a roasting pan and prepared his work station for tonight's dinner.

The rumble of a tractor and the scrape of a plow blade echoed in the still air and carried from the roadway. I stepped out onto the porch to listen to the hopeful sounds of our rescue. The plow still seemed distant on the county road leading to our drive, but it was reassuring to know work was in progress. Allen joined me on the porch while Luke frolicked in the snow. The snow had stopped falling but the temperature still registered in the teens.

"It will be hours before that plow reaches us, but at least it's a start. Nobody is leaving anytime soon," Allen commented. His hands rested on my shoulders. "I apologize for snapping at your earlier. Just wanted to save you from seeing that grisly scene."

I nodded and laid my head back against her shoulder.

"I'm sorry too; I should have listened to you. But Allen, how did Marlon Powers get here if the roads were closed? Who do you think killed him?" I asked.

I instinctively clutched Allen's arm as he drew me closer to him.

"That's the million-dollar question, isn't it? You've got to ask yourself, who benefits from his death?"

"Let's go inside and get something hot to drink if we're going to play twenty questions," I said.

We walked around the porch to the kitchen door, then deposited our coats in the mudroom. I noticed Claire's coat and gloves were missing. Perhaps Sally had returned the wet garments to her after they had dried. I'll have to remember to ask her.

Sally stood at the sink peeling a colander full of yams.

"Sally, please take Mrs. McConnell a cup of hot tea? She's in the living room. Thank you."

"Of course," she said as she wiped her hands and prepared the tea from the kettle always simmering on the stove.

After she left the room, I sat with Allen, Lucas, and Lionel at the table.

"I'd rather keep the news of Marlon Powers' death to ourselves for the time being. No need to start a panic among my guests; they have enough to deal with, being stranded in a snow storm," I said.

Allen's voice was low, clipped, the way he sounded when he was balancing both an investigator's duty and personal fear. Lucas kept pacing, his boots squeaking on the kitchen tile.

"We need a list of suspects," Allen said, finally dropping into one of my oak chairs. His hands clenched the edge of the table. "This wasn't an accident. Nobody ties a rope into a hangman's noose unless they mean for it to be used and seen."

Lucas nodded. "So who gains from Marlon Barlow being gone?"

I hugged myself; the heat of the kitchen not quite reaching the cold in my bones. "Margaret," I whispered. "His wife. And maybe one other."

"Who?" Lucas asked.

"Claire Jennings confided in me that she's in Clarkstown looking for her birth mother that gave her as a baby, over twenty years ago. Lionel did some research based on the scant information that Claire knew. He checked census records, marriage certificates, and birth records. Based upon what we found, we think Margaret Powers might be her birth mother."

"Wow! If that's true, would Claire want to kill her mother's husband?" Lucas asked as he scribbled notes.

Allen took up the discussion. "Hmm, what if Marlon had wanted the baby gone from the moment she was born? That might be the reason Margaret gave the baby away. What if he wasn't the father? If Claire discovered that fact or speculated her mother abandoned her because of him, that could be motive."

"I don't think Claire is strong enough to lift a body as heavy as Marlon. Also, from the dates we found online and from local gossip, which tends to be more detailed, Margaret went away to give birth and didn't marry Marlon until later. However, I think your suggestion that he wasn't the father is probably accurate."

"Well, if he found out that the girl was in town, she could be a threat to their standing in the area. A scandal would ruin the Powers' reputation. My money is on the wife. What if Marlon threatened her or Claire. Margaret could have been defending her child," Allen said as he dragged his fingers through his hair in a gesture I'd seen him do a thousand times. His mind rolled over facts and ideas, building a case.

"Did you find a second set of footprints in the snow?" Lionel asked as he chimed into the discussion.

"Hey, no, we didn't," Lucas answered in a voice barely above a whisper. "Holy cow!" His eyes widened at the implication.

"You still have the same problem ... how can a woman of Margaret's size or Claire's be able to lift a grown man? He had to be at least knocked out before being hanged or he'd fight back," I said and watched the two detectives mull over my supposition.

"If we rule out those women, who does that leave us with in the house? I think we can dismiss Tara McConnell, but her husband appears to be a strapping lad. That only leaves one of us to confess," Allen said.

Lucas scribbled notes. "Evan McConnell has been edgy the whole time we've been snowbound. He disappears for stretches."

"I hardly think Evan had any reason to kill Marlon. He's not even from this area. They live in Knoxville and were just driving through on their way to her parents home. I think as an expectant father, Evan has a right to be edgy. He's just nervous for his wife. Hey, y'all weren't serious when you suggested any of us were guilty, were you?" I asked, my eyes wide as I shot him a look.

"No, of course not."

I swallowed, my throat dry. "There's another possibility. One you can't write down in your notebook."

Allen gave me the look ... the one halfway between disbelief and concern. "Maddie..."

"I need to talk to you in private. Come with me," I said as I grabbed his hand and led him down the hall into my office. My research papers on my desk had been disturbed; someone had read them. My mind jumped to Claire but just as quickly I dismissed my suspicions as just that.

Closing the door, I turned to face Allen. He waited, his expression skeptical. How do I explain to this no-nonsense man that I've been living with a ghost?

"You better sit down. This may take a while. You may not believe me, but I swear that what I am about to tell you is the truth. When my grandmother, Polly Brooke, died two years ago, her ghost stayed in the inn. I can see her and talk to her. So can Lionel and Lily and now Tom. Of course Luke senses her."

"I don't believe in ghosts. What are you saying?"

"My Grannie is in this house. On this farm. Do you remember when you and I were searching for that secret door in the basement? It surprised you when I found it, but it was because my Grannie led me to it. Think back. There had to be times that made you wonder how I knew something that no one else could see."

"This is crazy. I deal in facts, not supernatural. But okay, for the sake of argument, let's suppose I believe you about your grandmother. What's that got to do with this current situation?" Allen asked.

"I'm telling you," I said, leaning forward, lowering my voice as if the walls themselves might eavesdrop. "An unworldly cataclysm occurred when lightning struck that elm tree. It released something. Grannie feels it too. There's another spirit here, an angry one. She's been fighting it, but she's not strong enough. You saw the words written on the window. Who do you think wrote that?"

As if on cue, a flicker passed through the lamps. Shadows stretched across the walls like long, crooked fingers. I shivered.

"I don't believe in ghosts. But I believe in you. Show me some proof, some kind of physical evidence to back up what you're feeling. I can't put ghost in a police report."

I nodded. I understood his policeman skepticism.

"But it's true! Believe it or not. I've seen him; felt him. Tara McConnell is having dreams about him ... premonitions ... visions that are too detailed not to be believed."

"What premonitions?" Allen asked.

"Claire told Lily and me that she was pushed down those stairs. Tara saw it in a dream. Who else but that evil ghost could have done that?"

"Great," Allen muttered. "So now we've got an invisible suspect."

# Chapter Seven

## Silas

"What are we going to do, Grannie?" I asked in a low voice as I took a moment of refuge in my office. Her translucent figure hovered near me. The inn seemed oddly silent.

Tara and Evan sat with Claire in the dining room playing a game of Scrabble, although I didn't think any of them had their minds on the game. Lionel and Lily huddled with Allen and Lucas at the farmhouse kitchen table discussing the storm and likelihood of leaving in the snow. Only Tom and Sally went about their normal routine, preparing the Christmas feast for later.

*"I've been wracking my memory of stories that occurred here on this farm, long before your Grandpa and I lived here. I seem to recall a tale about a midwife here at the farm, probably Charles grandmother, and a woman who died. Oh, I know, plenty of women died in childbirth back then, but this woman was rumored to have been murdered by her husband. She was expecting their child and he fought with her, or so the story went. If I'm right, it's his ghost that haunts us now. Silas Holt."*

"Did his wife die here? What was he doing at Magnolia Blossom?

There must be more to the story. Maybe if Lionel and I do some historical research we can learn the reason he's here," I said.

*"His soul is in agony. He wants revenge, but his time is past. The living now had no part in his lynching from long ago,"* Grannie said. *"Learn what you can. Search through that old box of newspapers that your Grandpa Charles kept in the basement. You might find what you want in there."*

Her image shimmered in the wintry light and then vanished.

I opened my laptop and searched for the name Silas Holt in the historical records of Albemarle County. Scribbling notes and dates on a scratch pad, I didn't hear Lionel step into the office.

"What are you doing? Can I help?" he asked.

My hand flew to my heart as I looked up. "Good gracious! You gave me a start. Yes, I can use your expertise. Grannie has given me a clue as to the identity of our mysterious spirit."

"No kidding. What are you looking into?"

"Historical records from around 1900. Grandpa Charles's grandparents were Albert Brooke and his wife Sara Leander Brooke. Family records listed Sara as a mid-wife."

"And you think maybe this mid-wife was somehow involved? Jeez, I feel like I've stepped into a Charles Dickens story," Lionel said.

"Grannie says she recalls hearing the story about Silas Holt killing his pregnant wife. It was one of those local legends that people whispered about over the decades. I thought that maybe a mid-wife here on the farm might have a connection why he was, uh, hanged here. I don't know. I'm grasping at straws."

"Well, let me get my computer and I'll see what I can find since we know the time period and names."

"Okay. I'm going to hunt through some boxes of old newspaper articles my grandpa saved. They're in the basement. I'll try and enlist the aid of Allen or Lucas to help me."

"You can try, but the guys said they were going back outside to cut down Marlon Powers' body. Allen has been trying to get a call into the county medical examiner. Don't think he's had any luck though," Lionel said.

"Good gracious! I just had a thought ... has anyone even tried to reach Margaret Powers to tell her about her husband?"

"Dunno. I suppose Allen might have called her."

We both left the office and returned to the kitchen. I saw Allen and Lucas heading toward the barn as I looked out the back door.

"What are they doing now?" I asked Tom as I pointed to the men trudging through the deep snow.

"Allen asked if there was a ladder in the barn and I told him yes, behind the stage platform. I guess they plan on climbing up to cut the rope holding the body. Can't very well allow him to stay swinging in the breeze," Tom said. He took a quick glance out the window at the snowy scene and then went back to dredging chicken in buttermilk and flour for tonight's dinner.

Lionel shuddered at Tom's words, then picked up his laptop and went back to the solitude of the inn's office where he could work privately.

Lily stepped into the kitchen and poured herself a cup of coffee. She moved over to the back door and stood with me as we watched our two men struggling to hoist the ladder in the snow. A few minutes later we saw them carry the body into the barn, where it would keep in the cold until the medical examiner arrived.

"I'm worried about Tara," Lily said as she sipped her coffee and stared out the window.

"Why? She seemed okay at breakfast."

"She's not resting. These dreams or premonitions that she's having are not good for the baby. I don't like it."

"I thought you'd be more concerned over Claire. Is she all right now? Has her head wound healed?"

"Claire is fine. Her wound was minor and the concussion was

short. Claire's problems are more mental than physical. She's obsessed with confronting her birth mother. I can't help but wonder what her situation has to do with the dead man out there. If her mother is really Margaret Powers, then what was her husband doing prowling the inn? Was he after Claire?" Lily asked. She frowned, producing tiny wrinkles on her brow and otherwise smooth skin.

"I'm sure they'll both be fine. They're in the hands of the most capable doctor in the county."

Lily smiled at me indulgently. "Thank you for such a glowing recommendation."

I squeezed her hand and smiled. "Guess I gotta go face the basement on my own, cobwebs and all. Ugh! I'll be back in either a few minutes or hours ... depends on how quickly I find what I'm looking for. You may have to send Lionel down to rescue me if I'm not back soon!" I said with a laugh.

Slipping on a heavy sweater, I started down the wooden stairs leading into our damp, chilly cellar. Grannie used to store her mason jars of canned tomatoes and green beans, plus jars of homemade jam down here. I hadn't done any canning since her passing, and now mostly dust, empty jars, and cobwebs filled the space. We have very industrious spiders in the South; they spin webs onto anything standing still or undisturbed. Now, as I descended into the lower level of the old farmhouse, I had to brush away the silky threads clinging to my hair and face as I moved among the boxes stored there.

Overhead, I could hear boots stomping, knocking off clinging snow, as Allen and Lucas returned to the house from their grisly chore.

Hmm, Grannie was right. Grandpa Charles kept every newspaper clipping that ever mentioned the Magnolia Blossom farm, whether good or bad press. I dug through a pile of dusty brown paper, setting aside articles from the fifties or sixties and searched in the bottom of the box for older dates.

Grannie's spiritual energy glimmered atop one of the boxes, pointing the way for me. I reached for the box and opened its seal.

Finally, I pulled out brittle newspapers from the turn of the century. Boldface print shouted a headline of MURDER. I skimmed the article and sat it on an empty shelf as I searched for additional stories. One short column article described the death of the culprit. Grabbing both news accounts, I shoved the box back onto the stack and then climbed the steps.

Hurrying into the office, it was my turn to startle Lionel from his deep concentration. I shoved the musty newspaper under his nose.

"Read this! It describes the murder of Abigail Holt and her unborn child and charges her husband Silas with her murder."

Lionel took the paper from my hand and began reading out loud:

"Silas Holt, a farmer in Clarkstown, Virginia was charged with the murder of his pregnant wife, Abigail, on December twenty-third, 1902. Neighbors reported a violent argument was heard between the couple, hours earlier before Abigail's bloody body was found lying near the brick hearth of the couple's small log cabin. Holt was arrested at the nearby farm of Albert Brooke where Holt said he had gone to get help from the midwife who lived there."

"Keep reading what it says about the trial," I interrupted Lionel and pointed to the next column.

Lionel cleared his throat and then read out loud again, "At the trial of Silas Holt, the local sheriff, Levi Powers, stated he had been at the Holt homestead on more than one occasion to settle altercations. The jury found Silas guilty. Silas Holt had no defense attorney. A vigilante group of citizens dragged Holt from his jail cell and strung him up from the tall elm tree near the scene of the crime." He stopped reading, then stared at me.

"Holy cow! It sounds like they railroaded the man," Lionel said.

"The article doesn't say how Abigail died, whether she fell and hit her head, or someone struck her. Her death could have been an accident or even a miscarriage."

"Did you notice the name of the sheriff? See if you can find out if Levi Powers was any relationship to Marlon Powers. Wouldn't that make for an interesting ghost story?" I asked.

Grannie popped into the room as we were talking. *"Prove Silas Holt was innocent of that crime so his spirit can be at peace. The towns-folk dragged him to that elm tree and hanged him after a mock trial. He swore with his last breath he'd curse every family who wronged him. His soul has twisted in that tree for generations until the lightning freed him."*

"There is definitely more here than meets the eye. We need more facts. A pity we can't interview anyone; there's no one still alive from that time frame. If we just had a diary or journal from someone who knew what really happened, or someone who could have testified in his behalf. This article makes it appear that the man never had a chance to explain what really happened. What if the argument the neighbors heard wasn't between Silas and Abigail? What if she was fighting with another man? She could have been assaulted." Lionel laid the paper on the desk and stared at me.

Lionel and his colleagues at the African-American Heritage Center constantly combatted this type of injustice. I could see the determination in his eyes.

"Come on. Let's share this information with Allen. He knows about the ghost from the tree. I'm not sure he believes in it, but I tried to explain Grannie and the appearance of this new spirit. Besides, Tom is fixing a delicious Christmas dinner tonight too. Nutritious food always makes things look better," I said as we joined the others in the kitchen.

Allen and Lucas stood talking to Tom. I studied their worried faces and wondered ... what now?

"We put the body in the barn," Allen said. His eyes hinted at something more.

I studied his face before a new idea popped into my mind.

"You think Marlon Powers rode that horse through the snow. That's it, isn't it? Claire mentioned seeing a car off the side of the road when she arrived. What would make Marlon so determined to get here that he'd steal a horse to make the trip?"

"I suppose it's one way to travel in a blizzard," Tom said.

"Either that, or his murderer did," Lucas said in a low voice.

My hand flew to my heart, and I raised wide eyes to him as I gulped at his words.

# Chapter Eight

## Christmas Eve

Christmas Eve at the Magnolia Blossom Inn should've been warm, golden, and full of cinnamon-scented laughter. Instead, it felt like a storm still raged inside the walls, despite the snow outside finally settling into silence.

The large parlor glittered from top to bottom in the late afternoon. Lionel had outdone himself with the music playlist—soothing crooners from the '40s, soft pop from the '60s, mingled with timeless carols that made the candles flicker in rhythm. Luke flopped near the fire; the big shepherd relaxed for the time being. My friends and guests mingled in clusters, with bourbon-laced eggnog or mugs of hot cider in hand.

"Dinner will be ready soon. Tom has outdone himself to cook you a traditional southern meal tonight."

I moved through the room with a tray of sugar cookies shaped like stars and snowflakes, the powdered sugar dusting my fingertips. Grannie drifted at my side, her Christmas-red shawl trailing mist. She was smiling ... until she wasn't.

Her head snapped toward the far side of the room.

*"He's here."*

"Who?" I murmured, careful not to spook the guests.

Her eyes, normally full of mischief, were sharp and troubled. *"The other one. The one that came with the lightning."*

A sudden draft slipped through the parlor, rattling the crystal ornaments on the tree. The air went cold enough to make my breath cloud. The McConnells looked around for the source, and Lionel muttered something about an old farmhouse and loose window frames.

But I saw it.

Not a full apparition ... just a ripple in the air, like heat above asphalt, except it felt icy. It drifted near the tree, where Claire sat stiff as a porcelain doll, hands folded so tightly in her lap, I thought she might snap her fingers. Sally squeezed Claire's arm in reassurance and smiled fondly at the young girl.

Luke's ears shot up. He gave a low, warning growl.

The ripple pulsed, then shot toward the tree.

The lights flickered.

Grannie's image shimmered in the corner. *"He's getting stronger. He's feeding off the emotional stress and fear of everyone in the inn."*

Ornaments swayed in the strong draft, tumbling off the tree onto the floor, like marbles pinging on glass. Someone screamed. I couldn't tell who, because my own voice had caught in my throat.

*"Leave us!"* Grannie's voice rang through the dark like a bell. The candles flared again, but the flames bent unnaturally toward the center of the room, as though being pulled.

I grabbed Lionel's arm. "Do you see—"

"Oh yeah. And I wish I didn't." His gaze locked onto the higher staircase landing. A shadow moved there ... tall, lean, and wrong somehow, as if it was a man but wasn't bound by skin or weight.

Claire jumped up, knocking over her chair. She bolted from the parlor, running into Allen. He caught her in his arms and steadied her. Lowering her head, she shuttered her angry eyes.

The cold withdrew in a snap. The room exhaled. Guests muttered nervously, clutching their drinks, trying to laugh it off.

Allen stood next to Lucas and stared at the damaged Christmas tree. He wore a perplexed frown.

"Electrical surge," Lucas suggested. "Probably from the ice."

But I knew better.

From the corner of my eye, I caught sight of a figure standing outside in the snow. He wore a dark coat, head tipped back as if watching the party through the window. My pulse hammered. The way he stood, too still, too patient ...

Grannie hovered close, her presence warm against the chill that lingered in my bones. *"His ectoplasm is getting stronger, Maddie. He can materialize now and he's not here to celebrate."*

Lionel handed me a glass of eggnog, though I wasn't sure if he meant to offer holiday cheer or comfort for my jangled nerves. My hand shook, sloshing the milky beverage over my fingers.

"Merry Christmas, huh?" he said with a half-smile.

I forced a smile. But all I could think was that whatever had come into the Magnolia Blossom tonight wasn't leaving without trouble.

I lit the candles in the center of the dining room table and on the pair of antique candelabra resting atop the mahogany sideboard to dispel my fears and provide a sense of holiday cheer, however false. The candle flames flickered on the long tapers. The dining room glowed with a warm welcome and festive look. An appetizing platter of deviled eggs sat at one end of the table with a basket of warm biscuits on the other. Everyone entered the room and took their same places at the table as before. However, the looks on their faces no longer held the merriment of the season ... this time their faces reflected wariness and fear.

Glancing at Allen, I silently beseeched him to do something to lighten the mood. He nodded, reading my expression, and tried to strike up a conversation with Evan McConnell.

"Guess you folks will be ready to get back on the road tomorrow if the plows finish. How far is it from here to Lancaster? Amish country. You know I used to live not far from there in Northeast Philadelphia," Allen asked.

Evan fidgeted in his seat, glanced at his wife, then tried to concentrate on the question asked of him. "Oh, yeah, I suppose so. Tomorrow. We've still got a four or five hour drive ahead, especially with the snow. Tara's parents are going to be disappointed that we aren't there tonight for Christmas Eve, but I'm sure they wouldn't want us to risk traveling in this mess."

"Better to play it safe," Lucas chimed into the conversation.

"Have you gotten through to them to let them know?" I asked.

Tara shook her head no.

Silence fell over the room again.

I clapped my hands; the sound echoed in the large room and was much louder than I had intended.

"Sorry. I'm going to help Tom and Sally serve. Be right back."

I dashed into the kitchen and began helping Tom arrange food onto plates. He really had outdone himself to provide the perfect meal to take our minds off our troubles. We plated crispy southern fried chicken on everyone's plates, added a spoonful of cornbread dressing filled with diced onions and celery, plus a scoop of candied yams. The gooey brown sugar and cinnamon spiced glaze coating the sweet yams was finger-licking good. Next came servings of a traditional green bean casserole and a Southern favorite ... tart yet sweet ...

a cranberry and pineapple salad. When the plates were brimming with food, Sally and I carried them into the dining room.

Tom joined us, and we all held hands and said a prayer of grace for the food and fellowship that we shared this night. I couldn't help thinking how much we needed that prayer tonight.

I raised my glass to make a short toast. "Merry Christmas to all our loved ones: families inherited or created and families formed through friendship."

"Hear, hear," Lionel chimed in.

Murmurs of appreciation floated around the table. I was happy to see that hungry appetites and delicious food helped to dispel the gloom and doom that had settled over our holiday celebration.

Polite chatter resumed amid bites of food.

"I heard plows on the road earlier, disappointed they didn't make it up your drive to clear us," Evan said.

"Sounds travel in this kind of weather; those plow trucks may have been miles from here. The major roadways demand immediate attention and then they'll get to the secondary streets," Tom said. He looked around the table at the anxious faces.

"At least we're all warm and comfortable. The generator has kept our electricity on, we've got plenty of delicious food thanks to Tom, and we're safe and sound," I said with a smile to everyone. My words fell flat, not inspiring confidence as I had hoped.

"Folks, I've got two special Christmas treats for dessert tonight. Take your pick of a rich pecan pie or a festive red velvet cake with a cream cheese frosting," Tom announced as he stood, hoping to tempt our guests with something sweet.

"Let me know your choice. Sally and I will ..."

Suddenly, Tara cried out, doubling over. Her hand clutched her belly.

The room fell quiet. All eyes turned to the pregnant woman.

Tara's eyes widened, and she looked frantically at her husband and then at Lily.

Lily slid her chair back and rushed to Tara's side. "Labor pains. It's a good thing you aren't on the roads in this snow. If y'all excuse us, this little lady is going to have a baby."

Evan supported his wife as she stood, then he and Lily each took an arm and helped her slowly climb the stairs to their room.

"Sally, go up and provide whatever the doctor needs ... towels, sheets, hot water. We'll take care of all this down here," I said. Sally nodded and took the stairs two at a time in her haste.

The men appeared uncomfortable with the idea of impending childbirth. Earlier, I had assured everyone that we were safe and sound here. But we all knew that *safe* was a relative term right now. Somewhere outside or even among us was a murderer. Plus, an evil spirit insisted on haunting the inn. And if all that wasn't enough, a baby had decided to enter the world on this night of all nights. Lily was an excellent doctor, but births can encounter complications that require a hospital. We could only pray that all goes well.

Allen and Lucas cleared the table while Tom took care of the left-over food. By mutual consent, we delayed dessert. I loaded the dishwasher and then straightened up the dining room table that we'd need for breakfast in the morning.

Claire retreated to the living room and curled into a chair near the fire, lost in her own thoughts and fears. I couldn't do anything for her right now. As I left the room, I caught a glimpse of her face in the mirror; resentment and anger reflected in her expression, then quickly masked when her eyes met mine. Did I imagine it? Perhaps the storm, the threat of an evil ghost, and a pending birth were playing tricks with my mind. I shook my head to dispel the thoughts.

"Lionel, will you please explain our research to Allen? Show him the articles and what you've found online. I'm going upstairs to assist Lily."

"Sure Maddie."

The men grouped around the big kitchen table, clutching bottles of beer and listening intently to Lionel's tales of civil injustice from long ago.

I entered the "sunflower" room where Tara lay in the middle of the bed. Her face was pale and sweaty, with her auburn hair plastered against her temples. She gasped and gripped her swollen belly. Her husband Evan sat near the side of the bed wringing his hands. Poor Evan already looked exhausted, yet the labor had just begun.

Lily appeared calm and in control. "Your contractions are getting closer. Reserve your strength, rest in between the pain. It's going to be okay."

Tara saw me standing by the door. She grasped Lily's hand as she panted, then relaxed. Her eyes were wild as she tried to speak.

"Maddie ... my dreams. I keep seeing him ... the man in the old clothes with hollow eyes. He stands in the corner of my room, waiting. In my vision, the baby's crying, and he looks ... pleased. Don't let him take my baby!"

"Those are just bad dreams. You're safe. No one will take your baby. We have two police officers in this house that will guard you, plus a doctor and your husband by your side. Put those thoughts out of your mind and just concentrate on the beautiful Christmas gift you'll soon have."

Grannie appeared in the flicker of candlelight. Her outline shimmered faintly, like snow caught in moonlight. She hovered near the bed, watching Tara's struggle to bring a new life into the world.

*"We've got to protect her from Silas Holt,"* Grannie whispered to me. *"In his vengeful mind, the baby is his."*

Her words made me more determined than ever to protect Tara and her baby and to solve the mystery surrounding Silas Holt.

# Chapter Nine

## Discovery

Grannie paced the floor in her own transparent way, floating above the furniture or passing through it. Lionel and I paced the room in tandem, sometimes bumping into one another as we passed. I wrung my hands and kept glancing at the clock, swearing the minute hand never moved.

*"Silas is getting stronger. Decades of rage have boiled forth giving him more substance to his spirit. He's dangerous. I'm afraid he'll harm someone, especially Tara,"* Grannie said.

"What can we do? We already found the newspaper articles about the so-called trial," I said.

*"It's not enough. Look deeper. What really happened to Abigail? Who was behind his wrong condemnation? Only the truth will free him."* Grannie said.

"I'll check courthouse records. Look at land transfers and public deeds. I'm curious to what happened to Silas's farm after he died. Maybe I can find something that makes sense," Lionel said.

Sally came rushing into the living room. She was out of breath from running. "Lily says she needs forceps, a tool she doesn't carry in her bag. I don't understand. She told me to ask you if the midwife had any."

Grannie stopped floating and pointed upstairs. *"Of course, Charles's grandmother Sara was a midwife. There may be a box in the attic of family heirlooms belonging to her. Look in there, Maddie."*

"Allen! I need you. Come with me and help me search. There's no time," I said as I grabbed his hands and we climbed the stairs to the third floor.

There were only two bedrooms on this floor, mine and Sally's. But under the eaves and dormers off the hallway were storage nooks. Small removable panels provided access to this attic space.

"What are we looking for?" Allen asked as he shined his flashlight into the cramped space.

"I'm not sure. Boxes from the turn of the century. Something with belongings of Sara Leander Brooke, a midwife back then. Lily is hoping she has some kind of tool that is used like forceps."

Since I was slimmer and could fit, I crawled into the dusty space and slid boxes toward the opening where Allen pulled them out and unsealed the lid, poking inside. We pushed each checked box back into the dormer space and then moved on to the next.

Dust motes swirled like a miniature tornado, shining in a shimmering light above the box. Grannie's mystical energy showed the way. In the second storage closet and fourth searched box, I found items that dated from 1900.

I backed out of the closet and dusted off my pants and sweater. Dust bunnies clung to my hair. This was not the holiday image and apparel that I had planned for Christmas. Self-conscious about my appearance, I shot Allen a look.

He laughed at the sight I made, then took his finger and wiped a spot of dirt off the tip of my nose.

"C'mon. Let's take this stuff downstairs."

Allen carried the box into the kitchen, placing it on the farmhouse table where we sorted through the contents in the brighter light.

Letters tied with ribbon, medical books, a small leather case of odd-looking tools, and several journals belonging to Sara L. Brooke were packed inside. We also found clothing, aprons and sleeve guards, and finally something that resembled forceps. I pulled out the tool and handed it to Tom.

"Boil this in a pot of water to sterilize it. Lily may need it."

Tom placed the ancient forceps into a deep pot of boiling water. I raised an eyebrow in wonder, but he merely shrugged.

"As soon as Tara went into labor, I started boiling water. That's what they always do in the movies," Tom said. I laughed. Why did I ever doubt the man? I could always count on him to be prepared for any emergency.

"I think I better get cleaned up. Lily won't want my dirty clothes and hands contaminating her delivery room. Give me fifteen minutes. Be right back," I said and then dashed upstairs to my room and bath.

Brushing my hair into place, I swept the long tresses to the top of my head and held them in place with a long decorative comb. Gold hoop earrings dangled from my ears and lent a holiday flair to my emerald green wool slacks and matching cable-knit sweater. A gold chain hung around my neck. I took a deep breath; now I felt more presentable for a Christmas Eve celebration at the inn. I wondered whether Allen would approve of the transformation.

Stopping at Tara's door on my way back downstairs, I looked in to see how things were progressing.

"How is she?" I asked Lily as I timidly approached the bed.

"Wow, look at you. So pretty." Lily commented on my change of attire. "Tara is doing well. She's taking a bit of a cat nap in between contractions. That's a positive thing. First babies take their time and she'll be here for a few more hours. In another ten minutes when the contraction hits, she'll be awake. Did you find any forceps? "

"Yes, I did. In the attic storage, which is why I had to get cleaned up."

"Great. I was hoping Grannie might know what I meant when I sent Sally down. Is Tom sterilizing the tool?"

"Sure is. They're boiling as we speak."

"I'm hoping I won't need them, but nice to have them on hand just in case," Lily said as she checked her patient's pulse.

I looked over at Evan. He had fallen asleep in the chair, still holding his wife's hand. Lily noticed where my attention fell and chuckled lightly.

"It's always worse on the husbands."

"Do you need anything? Can I bring you a coffee or tea?"

"I'd appreciate a cup of coffee," Lily said.

"Coming right up."

Back downstairs, I checked on Claire and offered her some more refreshments and then joined the gang in the kitchen. I fixed a cup of strong coffee for Lily, just the way she liked it, then asked Sally to take it up to the doctor.

Lionel nodded approvingly, while Allen softly whistled as I entered the kitchen.

"Approve?" I asked Allen.

"Maddie, you look lovely. Christmas personified," Allen said as he placed a kiss on my cheek and gave me a hug.

I needed that brief show of affection after all the horror of the past two days. For a brief moment, I melted into his embrace. It fortified me.

"We need to continue searching for more information about Silas

Holt. His spirit won't rest until we prove his innocence. I'm hoping this box might hold clues from the past," I said.

"You're still clinging to this belief that an evil spirit or ghost of some kind sprung out of that split tree. You expect us to believe that?" Allen asked. He dragged his hand through his rumpled hair.

"Yes, I do. Open your mind to the idea that there are souls that linger between our earthly world and beyond. Forces we can't explain but are there. I tell you it's true," I said with as much passion as I could. He had to understand.

We stood trying to read each other's minds, our eyes locked. My face reflected the anguish I felt, my faith in another level of existence. Finally, Allen sighed and looked away. He stared at the ceiling, around the room, and then out the window at the snowy winter scene.

"All right Maddie. Let's solve this hundred-year-old mystery and see if it puts your ghost to rest," Allen said. "What do we know so far, Lionel?"

Lionel flipped open his laptop screen. His fingers flew over the keyboard as he accessed courthouse records, deeds, and copies of wills. A long notepad contained his notes from previous searches.

"Okay, so far I've gone through land records dating from 1890 until 1940. I haven't gotten into more current records. It looks like Silas Holt owned a farm near here plus some fertile bottom land near the river. After he died, the farm and the title to that piece of land transferred to a Levi Powers. Powers appeared to be a wealthy mill owner and also held the position of local sheriff."

"So the same sheriff that arrested Holt gained the man's property after he was gone," Lucas restated the facts. His lawman's sixth sense twitched.

"Yeah, shady, huh?" Lionel said.

I fingered the stack of tied letters and picked up one of the journals written by Sara Brooke. She had kept a journal of her patients' names and the children born along with any medical problems associated with the births or mothers. Her meticulous record-keeping impressed me. I skimmed the pages until I found dated entries closer to the period in question.

"This is interesting. Look at this entry made on December fifteen, 1902, concerning Abigail Holt. That's about a week before her death. The midwife noted Abigail had experienced dizzy spells several times during that week and warned her not to lift anything heavy. To limit her work around the house to avoid light-headedness," I read.

"So it's possible that Abigail Holt might have become dizzy and fallen," Allen said as he scanned the journal.

He pointed to another entry made the day after Abigail died and the day Silas was arrested. I read the passage:

*"Sara wrote she went to attend to Abigail as soon as Silas came pounding on her door that frosty December morning. She found Abigail lying in a pool of blood; she had hemorrhaged with the baby dying in the womb. Abigail exhibited signs of a head wound and there was blood on the stone hearth. Sara concluded that the woman must have fallen in a dizzy spell and struck her head. She tried to testify at the trial, but the court forbade women."*

I put the book down and stared at the men. "Oh good gracious! A man died because this woman could not speak in court to defend him or explain his wife's death. How horrible!"

"That's how it was back then. Wasn't fair and it wasn't right, but sadly, it was a fact." Allen placed the journal on the table.

Lionel continued the tale as he recited trial records found online within the county historical archives.

"It seems this Sheriff Levi Powers testified he found Silas Holt with blood on his hands and therefore insisted that he had murdered his wife. No one disputed the accusation. The sheriff was the only witness at the trial. Holt was sentenced to hang for his crimes and a group of angry citizens took it upon themselves to carry out the deed. You know the rest."

Lucas had scribbled notes as we all pored over the gruesome details. He tapped his pen on the notepad. "So is this Levi Powers a relation to our corpse in the barn?"

Allen and I both raised eyebrows and looked to Lionel for an answer. He keyed in a data search and then nodded his head.

"Yep. Appears Marlon Powers is from the same family. His family wealth dates back to the turn of the century and the grain mill owned by Levi Powers. Spooky, isn't it. Hey ... do you suppose our ghost dude knew that? Could he have, uh ... you know?"

"Now you're stretching my imagination too much," Allen stated.

# Chapter Ten

## Joyous Noel

A crash echoed from upstairs ... a door slamming on its own. Lily shouted for towels. Tara screamed in pain. The clock in the hall struck midnight.

Christmas morning had arrived.

The icy wind clawed at the shutters like a wild animal, rattling the windows and hissing down the chimney. Every draft in the Magnolia Blossom Inn seemed alive, carrying whispers that weren't of this world. Upstairs, Tara's moans of pain echoed through the house as Lily worked confidently by her side. The remains of the snowstorm outside were fierce, but the storm inside ... the spiritual one ... was worse. I could feel it in the marrow of my bones.

"Stay calm, Maddie," Lionel murmured, his hand briefly squeezing mine as we stood at the bottom of the staircase. I had one foot on the step, ready to rush upstairs to lend assistance. His eyes, usually quick with humor, were dark and watchful. "We've got our friend's back. Lily's a rock."

All of a sudden, the chandelier overhead shuddered violently, crystal drops tinkling like brittle icicles. A bitter cold filled the hallway, so sharp I swore I smelled iron and smoke. I stopped my ascent and stared at the swinging light fixture.

Claire cried out and cringed, crumpling to the floor at the entrance to the parlor. Her hands covered her ears as she whimpered in terror.

Grannie appeared at the foot of the stairs, her presence shining like lantern light in the gloom.

*"He's here,"* she said, her voice tight. *"Silas. He's after the child."*

My heart lurched. "Why? What would he want with a baby?"

Before Grannie could answer, a low growl rolled through the walls. Every candle, every light bulb flickered out, plunging us into darkness, except for the silver glow clinging to Grannie. And then I saw him, clear as day and as solid as anyone. Silas Holt. His gaunt figure materialized, reflected in the hallway mirror, dressed in a torn coat from another century. Rope burns etched deep lines into the shadow of his throat. His eyes blazed with anguish and fury, but beneath it, I thought I saw sorrow.

Allen and Lucas exchanged looks of disbelief. I knew they were witnessing Grannie and the other ghost.

*"She was mine!"* His voice split the air like lightning. *"My wife! My child! You can't have them!"*

We all heard his words of agony.

Grannie stepped forward, radiant but trembling. *"Silas Holt, you were wronged ... but this path isn't yours. It's not your wife and child here tonight. Let them be."*

The walls shook. Upstairs, Tara screamed again, the sound tearing through me. Lily's voice was urgent, commanding, telling her to push, to breathe. We heard Evan offering words of encouragement and comfort. The old elm tree outside groaned in the storm's aftermath, its shattered limbs scraping the house like bony fingers.

Grannie spread her arms wide, as if she could block the entrance of the staircase.

Silas surged forward, and the temperature plummeted. My breath came out in clouds. Lionel grabbed my arm to steady me, whispering, "We can't fight him like this."

But then Grannie turned to me, her eyes shining. *"Love, Maddie. Call on it. All of you. Together."*

"Everyone!" I cried, my voice shaking but loud. "Hold on to each other. Think of Tara and her baby. Think of our friendship and our love for each other. Feel the love of your families and capture those memories. Hold tight to those feelings. Pray to God to protect us tonight from evil."

Tom and Sally, Lionel, Lucas, even Claire gathered in the parlor with me and Allen at the foot of the stairs, clutching hands, blocking Silas. We made a human chain with Grannie in the center of the circle. The warmth of our spirits spread like fire through my veins. I held onto Allen and gazed at Grannie, pouring every memory I had of Christmas mornings, laughter around the tree, my grandparents' love, and the loyalty of friends into our united circle. Our hands locked together securely.

The glow around Grannie blazed brighter, swelling with our strength. She lifted her hands before her, and Silas reeled back, his form flickering.

"Silas Holt," I cried in a commanding voice, "you were innocent of your wife's death. We know you were betrayed. Your story will be told. I promise you. I'll find the historic records to prove your innocence. But you cannot stay here and harm the living."

For one instant, his eyes locked with mine ... storm-gray, filled with grief. A husband, a father-to-be, crushed by injustice. Then he screamed, the sound rattling the rafters, and his figure tore apart like smoke in the wind, swept out into the night.

"Wow! I wouldn't have believed it if I hadn't seen it," Lucas said.

"Tell me what I just saw was real," Allen said in a low voice.

Silence filled the room, broken all of a sudden by the ragged cries from above. Then ... a baby's lusty wail. Strong, defiant, beautiful.

Tears stung my eyes as relief broke through the tension. Lionel let out a shaky laugh. "That's one way to enter the world, huh?"

Grannie sagged, her glow dimming. I rushed to her side, but she managed a smile. *"It's all right, child. He's gone ... for now. But remember your promise. Find the truth. Clear his name. Only then will he truly rest."*

I nodded, my throat tight. "We will, Grannie. Lionel and Allen and me. We'll dig until we find all the facts."

The others squeezed my hand in silent vow, the circle of love still strong. Above us, Lily's voice rang out, tired but joyful:

"It's a girl. Merry Christmas, everyone."

Voices raised in cheer, in relief, and in our faith of a higher being that had protected us in love.

Within the inn, light and warmth glowed along with the newest heartbeat of hope ... baby Noelle.

# Chapter Eleven

## Christmas Day

The Magnolia Blossom Inn had never felt so alive. Despite the exhaustion from the previous long night, joy rang through every room. From the kitchen drifted the aroma of cinnamon streusel and baked apples. Tom hummed to himself as he cooked a holiday breakfast deserving of a four-star Michelin culinary rating. In the living room, the scent of pine garland and Fraser fir mingled with beeswax candles that still glowed in their silver holders.

Upstairs, Tara McConnell cradled her newborn daughter, her face luminous though pale. Lily hovered nearby, fussing over the baby as a caring physician with her first obstetrics case. Evan had the chore of packing their car in readiness for the journey.

Allen Crawford and Lucas Wampler sat at the dining table, steam curling from their untouched mugs of coffee. Their notebooks lay open, the pencil scratches of a long night of speculation already filling the pages.

"Are we going to discuss what happened last night? I mean, I was there, but I can't believe it was real. I'm afraid to admit it," Lucas said in a low voice, glancing over his shoulder.

"Yeah, I know what you mean. Maybe it was really mass hypnosis, like we were under the influence of some kind of drug ... the power of suggestion or too much bourbon in that eggnog. I don't believe in the supernatural, yet I hesitate to label what we witnessed either. Maddie will swear her grandmother's ghost is in this house and that she fought against an evil spirit that threatened all of us. It's the most farfetched story I've ever heard and yet I was here," Allen said.

"Well, yeah, but ..."

"No butts. Let's get down to business in the only way I know how. Facts. We need to concentrate on the facts. When we get back into the office, maybe this will all make sense," Allen stated.

Allen tapped the end of his pencil against the table. "So. Let's lay it out clean, Lucas. Marlon Powers, hanged from that elm tree. Initial thought, a suicidal lynching. But ..."

"... the rope," Lucas cut in, flipping a page back. "Not frayed, not weathered. Fresh hemp, cut by a sharp knife. Knots too neat. He didn't tie that himself during the storm."

Allen nodded grimly. "And the footprints. One set going toward the tree, not away. Which means somebody else left the scene by another path."

Lucas leaned back, running a hand through his hair. "We overlooked the broken lantern near the barn door. Found it this morning, half-buried in snow. Oil spilled around it. Whoever carried it, might've been meeting him there before it all went bad."

Allen closed his notebook with a snap. "We're not finished here," he murmured. "Not by a long shot."

From the sitting room came the sound of Lionel plunking randomly at the piano, trying to dispel the shared nightmare with carols, though the notes faltered when his thoughts drifted. I sat nearby, humming in harmony. The warm circle of new life and old friendships knitted together the night's frayed nerves.

Grannie hovered nearby. Her translucent image rested near the story Christmas tree, barely visible in the rays of light filtering through the large bay window. Her ghostly energy waned, fatigued from the battle waged with Silas Hot.

From outside came a low rumble ... the steady churn of snowplows at last making their way down the inn's long drive. Relief swept through the household like a spring thaw. The storm had broken; the roads were opening. Christmas morning sunlight streamed through the frosted panes, turning every icicle into a prism of light. I could hear cheers from upstairs as others heard the plows and realized it meant freedom.

The guests gathered in the large front hall, coats buttoned and bags packed. Voices carried that strange blend of fatigue and relief that follows surviving a tremendous storm. The end of a strange reunion of sorts, unexpected yet filled with powerful feelings. Murmured goodbyes, expressions of gratitude, unspoken words of the mystical ordeal endured lingered in the air.

Smells of coffee and cinnamon streusel, plus Tom's Christmas morning breakfast extravaganza aroma permeated the inn. One last holiday ritual was shared to keep spirits high before the exodus began.

"You keep that baby warm," Lily spoke softly as she touched the smooth skin of the tiny cheek. She pressed a kiss to the top of the baby's head and marveled once more at the thrill of bringing a new life into the world. "I'm going to miss this little gal. Now you promise me you'll stop and take breaks; you've just given birth and you need to rest."

She wagged her finger at Evan. "Don't get to Lancaster by speeding; these roads are still slippery. You'll get to your parent's home soon enough."

"We promise," Evan and Tara said simultaneously, then laughed. Tara hugged the baby tight against her chest. Tiny Noelle lay snugly wrapped in a knit blanket I gifted her from the inn's collection.

Tara hugged Lily, their eyes held. "Thank you!"

Lily nodded and wiped a tear from her eye.

Lucas and Allen stood witnessing the emotional farewells. Lucas whispered in Allen's ear, "Is it wise to let them leave? They are part of our murder investigation, right?"

Allen nodded to Lucas and then stepped forward.

"I'll need a phone number where I can reach you both in Pennsylvania. Just routine. Drive safely now," Allen said as he shook Evan's hand.

"I, uh, gave Maddie our parent's phone number," Evan replied. He met the detective's gaze and nodded.

"Okay then."

"Keep in touch and let me know the baby's progress. Maybe you folks can swing by here again on your way back to Knoxville after the new year," I suggested.

"Uh, maybe," Evan gulped. His hesitant voice filled with memories of the holiday horror and ghostly terror still fresh in his mind.

We stood on the porch— Lionel, Lily, and I— and waved goodbye to the McConnell family as they cautiously drove down the long snow-packed drive. Tara had finally gotten through to her mother on the phone; I could still hear her eager exclamations over the birth of tiny Noelle and her joy to learn they would arrive by Christmas night. They had not missed Christmas with their family; it had only been delayed.

"I'm glad they got off okay. Hope they arrive safely," I said.

Luke romped and played in the cold air, jumping into deep snowdrifts and tunneling out the other side. Prissy marched across the porch, her kitten Mickey close behind, as she shook her fur and assumed reign over her realm. A cardinal dared to perch on the porch railing but flew off shrieking when Prissy meowed a warning.

I shook my head as I watched; the animals celebrated their liberation from being shut into the house. Rubbing my hands up and down my arms to take off the chill, I nodded toward the kitchen door. Lionel and Lily both followed me back into the warm house. Tom was already pouring fresh hot coffee for us.

"Where's Sally?" I asked Tom.

"She's still upstairs with Claire. Guess she's helping her pack or something. Those two really hit it off. Sally seems to have taken Claire under her wing like a younger sister. Kinda nice."

"Yes, it is. I didn't realize how lonely Sally must be feeling with her son far away over the holidays. What kind of friend am I that I didn't notice?" I said in a low voice, hanging my head.

Lily wrapped an arm around my shoulders and gave me a hug. "The kind of friend that has been taking care of a house full of people, making sure everyone was safe even when faced with unknown forces."

I looked up at her and swallowed back the emotion building at the back of my throat. "Thanks. It's important to be surrounded by dear friends, my family, at a time like this."

The sound of another vehicle inching its way up the drive caught our attention. Tom held back the cafe curtain on the kitchen window and glimpsed a red BMW pulling in. He whistled appreciatively at the sleek vehicle.

Footsteps sounded on the wooden porch floor, then a quick knock before the front door creaked open. Wind carried in a spray of snowflakes, causing the holiday garlands on the balustrade to swing.

On the threshold stood a woman swaddled in a heavy fur coat, her hood partially covering her face. Cheeks flushed red from cold or emotion; difficult to say.

"Hello?" she called out.

I moved to the foyer, where Allen joined me to greet the woman. Allen scrutinized the person, making a quick decision.

"Margaret Powers," Allen said under his breath, his eyes skimming her appearance.

She stepped forward, scraping her boots on the mat. Her leather-gloved hands trembled as she clutched her coat tighter.

"Yes, I'm Margaret Powers. I came as soon as I could get out after the blizzard." Her eyes darted around the room, frantic, searching. "Where is my husband? Tell me Marlon is here. I saw his car in a ditch alongside the road." She looked at me then turned to Allen. "Who are you?"

"Detective Allen Crawford of Charlottesville PD. What makes you think he would be here?" asked Allen.

Margaret fidgeted, her head hung low, then she raised her eyes to face the detective. "We had a terrible argument a few nights ago and he stormed out of the house. He threatened to take care of my, um, past mistake, as he called it. He, uh, meant my child. We heard her name in town and that she was staying at the inn for Christmas. I'm afraid he intended to harm the girl. I came to ... find out if, uh, all was well."

Silence filled the inn like a sudden frost. Allen's jaw tightened, but he spoke with measured calm. "Mrs. Powers, we need to talk. We discovered your husband dead yesterday morning."

Margaret's breath hitched, and she swayed against the doorframe. I crossed the space to gather the distraught woman into my arms. Helping her out of her heavy things, I led her to a comfortable chair in the living room.

"We better come in here to talk," I said.

"How? How did he die? Can I see him?" She gazed frantically between me and the detective.

"He's gone, Margaret," I whispered. "I'm so sorry."

Margaret's face twisted, grief and something sharper flashing across her features. "I warned him. I told him not to come here. He was obsessed ... obsessed with finding Claire."

# Chapter Twelve

## Reunion

The name struck the room like a match to tinder. From the staircase came a sharp gasp. Claire, pale as parchment, clutched the banister, her eyes wide and wet. Sally stood by her side.

"Margaret? Are you my mother?" She whispered, her voice trembling.

Margaret froze, her face crumpling in disbelief. "Claire?"

In an instant, Claire flew down the remaining stairs, tears spilling forth. Margaret sprang to her feet. Claire collided into the older woman's outstretched arms. Margaret wrapped her daughter in a desperate embrace.

"My baby," Margaret sobbed, burying her face in Claire's hair. "I thought you were lost to me forever. That I'd never be able to see you or claim you."

"You left me," Claire accused, voice muffled against her mother's shoulder. "All those years, I thought you never wanted me. I've searched for you."

Margaret pulled back just enough to cup Claire's face, her hands trembling. "My poor child. I was forced to give you up. I had no choice."

"Why? I think I deserve to know why you abandoned me," Claire shouted in a voice suddenly strong and demanding.

Margaret sank onto the sofa, pulling Claire down next to her. She glanced around the room at the rest of us who had gathered to hear her story.

She covered her face with her hands, then dropped them into her lap. Margaret took a deep breath, and in a low voice, began her story.

"Oh dear. How do I begin? It was springtime; I had just celebrated my sixteenth birthday. There was a St. Patrick's Day party and dance in town that I attended with a girlfriend. I was young and coquettish, daring to experience what it was like to be with a boy. My parents didn't allow me to date at that age, but since the party was well-chaperoned by church elders, they considered it safe for me to go."

She paused in her story and studied Claire's face. I could see her mind going back in time, perhaps recalling the features of a certain young man Claire resembled.

I brought a tray of hot tea with a plate of Christmas cookies and set it on the table by the sofa. Pouring cups for Margaret and Claire, I waited with the others for Margaret to resume her tale. Lily and Lionel quietly sat in the side chairs next to me; Allen propped his hip on the armrest of my chair with his arm draped across the back. Lucas stood in the doorway; his forehead creased as he listened.

"Johnny asked me to dance. He was handsome and charming with a twinkle in his eye and he made me laugh. We danced together the entire night, only pausing to take some punch and cookies for refreshment. I was smitten immediately. When he offered to walk me home, all I could think of was holding his hand and spending more time with him," Margaret said. She sipped her tea and studied the face of the girl next to her.

"You're very much like him. I see him in your eyes and the shape of your nose. Needless to say, when my father saw the young man on his doorstep, he forbade him to come back. Johnny didn't move in the same social circles as my family. My father declared he wasn't good enough for me. But what did they know? All my parents cared about was social standing; they didn't care about me or my feelings.

"They shut me into my room; only allowed to attend school during the day and forbidden to go elsewhere. I was miserable and determined to see Johnny again so my friend Elsie plotted with me to fool my parents. She invited me to her home for a weekend of Bible study and church on Palm Sunday. My parents agreed. Elsie got word to Johnny and he secretly met me there. We spent that entire weekend together. I was sure I loved him as only a young teenage girl can do, foolish and naive. He told me he loved me and wanted to marry me and I gave myself to him. I'll never know whether it was just a line he gave me to take advantage of me or if he really meant it. Word got back to my mother that Elsie had lied and I wasn't at her house. When I returned home, my mother loaded me onto a train for Atlanta to stay with my aunt. She thought distance and time would cure my lust for the boy. She was mistaken. A month later I realized I was pregnant."

"Oh no! What did you do? Did you stay in Atlanta or go home?" Claire asked. She bit her nails, hanging on every word, not interrupting until now.

Glancing at Grannie floating above the corner of the room, I already knew the answer to that question. I waited to hear what Margaret was going to say.

"My family insisted that I get an abortion. My mother told me to stay in Atlanta until I took care of the problem. But I couldn't. How could I kill my baby? Johnny's baby? I cried for days and days until my aunt relented and agreed that I could live in Georgia until the baby was born but that I had to give it up for adoption. That was my only option or risk scandalizing my family."

Claire hugged Margaret. Both women wore looks of anguish and grief. A mother and daughter torn apart. Years lost. The room was silent. What could we say after hearing such a tragic story?

Margaret continued her story. "When I returned from my aunt's, my father introduced me to Marlon Powers. Marlon had enlisted in the Army but his family stood among Clarkstown's elites and possessed money. The marriage was arranged immediately and then Marlon's unit deployed overseas. After he returned, we built a life in Clarkstown. The irony of course, was that I was never able to conceive after your birth. The doctor had told me that because I was so young, I'd had a difficult delivery and had likely damaged my body. Perhaps it was for the best."

I wiped a stray tear from my eyes after listening to her sad tale. Glancing at Lily, I saw my friend felt the same. I swallowed the lump in my throat as Margaret continued explaining to Claire.

"Knowing your adoptive parents loved you and you had a happy home meant everything to me. I never forgot you. I've kept track of you over the years. You were always in my mind and heart. Please forgive me." Her voice broke, tears sliding down her stained cheeks.

"It wasn't enough," whispered Claire.

I frowned, wondering if anyone but me had heard her.

The women clung to each other, crumpling onto the sofa, as everyone gazed on.

Lionel and Lily unobtrusively slipped out of the room after witnessing the scene before them. Lionel whispered to Lily, "Another Christmas miracle."

She nodded to him, her own eyes misty.

Allen and Lucas exchanged a long look across the room. The emotional reunion was powerful, but for them it raised more questions than answers. If Marlon had sought Claire here at the inn, with secrets buried for decades, who else might have wanted him stopped and to keep those secrets silenced? Who was this Johnny fellow?

Lucas nodded, eyes flicking to Margaret and Claire clinging to each other, grief and love binding them together in the glow of the Christmas tree.

Later, Margaret Powers sat stiff-backed on the settee, her gloved hands clasped tight. Claire Jennings, uncertain, waited across the room. Her packed bag was at her feet. For a long moment, no one breathed.

Then Margaret whispered, "Claire ... come home with me?" Her voice cracked, not with weakness but with a trembling humiliation that seemed foreign to her otherwise proud bearing.

Claire's shoulders shuddered as she let out a breath and nodded a tearful yes. At long last, mother and daughter were united.

"We'll need to speak to you again, máam. I still have questions concerning your husband's death. Also, the medical examiner will have your husband's body for a few days. His office will call you when it can be released for burial," Allen said in a firm tone.

Margaret nodded solemnly.

"All right. I understand. Are we free to leave?" Margaret asked.

"Yes máam. But please don't leave the area."

Allen and Lucas watched the women walk down the snowy path toward the car.

"There go our two best suspects," Lucas said.

"Maybe, but we know where they'll be. However implausible, you can be sure Powers' death is connected to them somehow," Allen said, then turned and walked into the kitchen.

Lily and I stood on the porch, side by side, saying our farewells to the two women as they climbed into Margaret's BMW. I had promised to return Claire's rental car for her tomorrow in Clarksville.

We hurried back into the house and joined the others in the cozy kitchen. Allen and Lucas welcomed us with open arms. After witnessing such an emotional outpouring, I felt drained and thankful for the pair of comforting arms holding me tight. I think we all got caught up in her story. It made me wonder what would have happened if Marlon Powers had confronted Claire. Would he have carried out his threat?

Lionel waited patiently in the kitchen with Tom, drinking a last cup of coffee. I smiled at the two men in my life who were always there to help me.

"Good gracious, we never even got to exchange our Christmas gifts," I said. "This holiday has been such a disaster."

"Maybe we should wait to do it later, in a few days after things settle down," Lily suggested, seeing my disappointment. "Sorry, but I've got to leave. I have patients to check on and have been away from the office far too long."

"Hey, how about we all get together for New Year's Eve?" Lionel said with a big grin. "Ready Lily? I'll go warm up the car."

I heard tires crunching on our plowed driveway. The medical examiner's van had arrived. Allen and Lucas donned their coats and boots and prepared to meet the M.E. from Charlottesville. Everyone stood on the back porch saying awkward goodbyes while eyeing the personnel making their way into the barn.

Allen shook his head. He was sorry to leave too, but his holiday dinner invitation had stretched into three days, and he had an investigation to run.

Lucas gave Lily a long, lingering kiss with a smile that said he'd see her soon. I raised my eyes to Allen, waiting, wanting. He complied with a brief kiss and quick caress that I wished had taken longer.

"I've gotta go. I'll call you. C'mon partner, let's go talk to these guys." He strode toward the barn with Lucas close behind.

I nodded and watched him, listening to the voices carrying in the crisp wintry air.

"Whatcha got for me, Crawford?" asked one of the attendants.

"Marlon Powers, age 44, hanged on the 24th. Lucas and I cut him down from that elm tree you see in the back. The one that's all black and split in half from a lightning strike."

"Hmm, that's a hell of a Christmas tale. Sounds like a Charles Dickens' story," the medical examiner said.

Two attendants lifted the body onto a gurney, placed it inside a black body bag and zipped it up.

"Okay boys, let's roll. I'll call you tomorrow after I've done my post mortem."

"Thanks, Doc," Allen said.

Luke barked and bounded off the porch into the barnyard as the vehicles pulled away. Silence finally reigned.

# Chapter Thirteen

## Suspects

Later that day, in the solitude of the Charlottesville police station, Detectives Allen Crawford and Lucas Wampler sat across from one another at the evidence table. Marlon Powers' case file lay open between them, papers scattered like fall leaves.

"No footprints beyond the ones we followed near the barn," Allen said, rubbing his temples. "But we did later find a second set leading from the elm tree toward the orchard. Smaller stride, lighter weight."

"Could be Claire's," Lucas offered. "Could be someone else entirely. Margaret claims she only traveled that morning after the plows went through, but neighbors in Clarkstown can't vouch she was or wasn't near the inn before that."

Allen grunted. "That leaves Evan McConnell. He had no reason to hate Powers. He didn't know the man that I can see. I agree he acted nervous and disappeared outside a couple times, but Tom told me he caught the man sneaking a cigarette. He had promised his wife he'd quit and was hiding it from her. Once Tara went into labor, he stayed upstairs. Lily vouches for him being with his wife the entire time. And then there's Margaret herself ... she could have been defending her child. She said Marlon threatened Claire. Although Margaret appeared to be surprised by his death."

Lucas leaned back in his chair. "Unless she's a better actress than we gave her credit for."

They had stopped at the Powers' residence before driving back to Charlottesville. The widow had taken to her bed pleading a migraine, but Claire had let them in. He and Lucas searched Marlon's office but avoided the rest of the house for the time being. They were in and out in less than an hour.

Allen emptied the confiscated brief case onto the desk top. He sorted through the enclosed stack of papers, then passed three interesting letters to Lucas.

"Well, well. According to these letters, we may have a new motive. Looks like he had business disputes, debts he never settled. At least two men in town had cause to want him gone," Lucas said.

"Plenty of cause," Allen admitted. "But opportunity? That storm had everyone pinned down tight." He tapped the file. "And then there's the strangest possibility of all."

Lucas raised an eyebrow. "You're not really entertaining Maddie's theory, are you? That the ghost of Silas Holt had a hand in this? I thought you didn't believe in the supernatural."

Allen sighed, closing the folder with a snap. "I don't like it. But I can't ignore the timing ... the lightning-struck tree, Tara's reported visions, and can you explain what we witnessed on Christmas Eve? Were we all hallucinating from something we drank in the eggnog? Consider the history between the Powers and Holt families ... and then Powers ends up hanging from that same elm. It doesn't fit any logical pattern I know."

Lucas gave a half-smile. "So we're down to suspects living and dead."

The phone rang, a jarringly loud sound in the still room. Allen answered the call in one-syllable words and grunts. He nodded to himself and scribbled a few notes. When he hung up, he scratched his beard and stared at Lucas.

"That was the M.E. He found head wounds on Powers. Said that was the cause of death, not strangulation."

"Whoa ... if he got clobbered in the head, then why hang him? To make a point? What if the person who hit him wasn't the same person who put him in that tree?" Lucas said, his pen drawing doodles as he spoke. He glanced down and saw he had drawn a hangman's noose around a stick figure.

"This just complicates the case even more," Allen said.

They still had no suspects they could positively name. The living offered only half-truths and grudges, but in the corners of their minds lay that uneasy thought neither could quite dismiss. Perhaps the storm had brought more than snow. Perhaps Silas Holt had reached across the years and taken his revenge at last.

At the inn, long after the last car, truck, and plow had disappeared down the road, I found myself alone in the office library. Tom had left to go home and check on his own house following the storm. Sally had retreated to her room to rest. Luke slept at my feet, tail twitching in some dream. Prissy meowed from the corner of the daybed where she had curled up. The lamplight flickered across yellowed papers spread on the desk—Sara Brooke's diary from 1902.

Her penmanship was elegant but sorrowful.

"The Powers family grows darker by the year.

They won their land through deception, and poor Silas
Holt still bears the town's hatred for a crime he did
not commit. Abigail's death was no accident, nor his
punishment just. The noose took him beneath the great
elm, and his spirit lingers in unrest."

I shivered, tracing the ink with my fingertip. Sara had known. Sara had written it plainly over a century ago.

Stretching my arms above my head, I forced myself to get out of the snuggly warm bed and start my day. Sunshine glistened on the snowy fields and streamed through my window. The inn was as silent as a grave with only Sally and me in the house. Yesterday we had taken care of stripping all the bedding from the guest rooms, and today would be just a matter of making the beds with the freshly laundered sheets and putting things to right.

I had promised Claire I'd drive her rental car back into town and drop it off since she went home with Margaret. She didn't need the car any longer; there wasn't any sense in paying for a daily rental. Sally would have to drive our truck into town with me or swing by to pick me up later.

Dressed in comfortable jeans, a pullover turtleneck, and a heavy wool sweater over that, I slipped my feet into a pair of waterproof hiking boots and headed downstairs. I made a pot of coffee and started scrambling eggs for Sally and me as I heard her moving about in the laundry room.

"Good morning. How about some breakfast? Feels funny with

the house empty after so many people here over Christmas. Doesn't it?"

"It's definitely quiet. I haven't decided whether or not I like it. I kind of miss Claire. Hope she's getting on all right with that woman. Did you believe her story, about why she abandoned Claire as a baby?" Sally asked, pouring herself some orange juice and setting out two plates and silverware on the table.

"Yeah, I did. She sounded genuinely regretful. I think she was afraid of her parents as a young girl and then her husband later. Hey, I promised Claire I'd return that rental car today. But I'd like to nose around the newspaper office and local records in the library or city hall. If I drive that car into town, can you swing by and pick me up later? I was going to have you follow me, but I don't know how long I'll be."

"Why don't you call me when you're about done and I can come into town to get you? That will give me time to finish the laundry and make up the rooms," Sally said.

"Okay. Perfect. I need to find some facts that aren't shown online and there's no better place than the archived stacks of an old newspaper office."

The Clarkstown Gazette office smelled of old paper and dust, the kind that clung to your clothes no matter how short the visit. Sally would have refused to step inside without an apron and a mop, but I found the scent strangely comforting. History had its own perfume ... ink, time, and secrets.

Mr. Bell, the Gazette's editor, had unlocked the archives for me earlier that morning, waving me toward the back room with only a muttered, "Don't spill coffee on anything." Gracious! I didn't even have a thermos with me.

He was gruff, but I knew he liked the idea of me poking into old society pages. He was used to my historical explorations during my school years.

Glancing at my watch, I saw I'd been digging through dusty papers for over two hours but had found nothing yet. I flipped through the bound editions of 2002, the headlines a jumble of budget debates, local football triumphs, and county fairs. Then I found it ... March 9th, 2002, the society wedding of the season.

**Margaret Quinton Marries Marlon Powers in Elegant Ceremony.**

The write-up went on about Margaret's lace gown imported from Richmond, the magnolia blossoms in her bouquet, and the prominent families in attendance. I scanned the list of groomsmen and bridesmaids: acting as maid of honor, a cousin from Crozet; bridesmaid Elsie Ward; groomsmen two Powers uncles; and as best man, Marlon's brother from Charlottesville. My eyes narrowed at the reception details.

And then I saw it. A single line, almost a throwaway...

*"Among the out-of-town guests noted for their charm upon the dance floor was Johnny Wiley, a friend of the bride."*

My heart gave a little skip. Johnny Wiley. Could he be the Johnny Margaret had talked about? Would she have invited him invited to the wedding, or did he dare to crash the reception? The Wiley name carried some weight in Clarkstown. His brother Joe owned and managed the hardware store on Main Street. Everyone trusted Joe; I considered him a dear friend. If Johnny had once been Margaret's sweetheart, then Claire Jennings' roots might entwine two local family trees.

Still, another part of me wondered, could it have been John Kelce instead? The Kelces were farmers. Honest and hardworking folks, certainly not wealthy. Like most farmers, they earned an average income. Their land bordered the northern pastures of Magnolia Blossom. Jeb Kelce was a respected, but stubborn man. If his younger brother John had courted Margaret, there might be clues buried somewhere deeper in the Gazette files.

I chewed the end of my pencil as I jotted names on my notepad ... Wiley or Kelce ... both possible. Both dangerous if Marlon had ever suspected one of them. I needed to mull the information over in my mind. Maybe Allen would be interested in looking into the backgrounds of both men.

Setting aside the 2002 volume, I reached higher on the shelf, tugging down the bound papers from 1902. I needed to dig further into the past. These pages were brittle, their headlines blaring with the bold strokes of another era.

**Local Farmer Hanged in Mob Justice**

The name sent a shiver through me. Silas Holt. Accused of murdering his wife, Abigail, after a violent quarrel. The sheriff at the time, Levi Powers, had led the men who chased Silas Holt onto Brooke land, finally catching him. They dragged Silas to the elm standing next to the barn and lynched him. I traced the grainy photograph of the tree, its stark branches stretching across the faded newsprint. This was the same information that we'd found during our online search. After Silas Holt died, Powers acquired all the land owned by Holt. In today's world, that act would have been highly suspicious, but back then it was a tight-knit community and the sheriff ruled.

Still, I had promised Silas Holt that I would clear his name, and I planned on keeping my word. I had to dig deeper. Grannie would expect me to keep looking and piece the puzzle pieces together.

I sighed as I slid the brittle pages back into the file. But then another article, printed a week later, caught my eye. I tugged the paper out of the folder and read a surprising account.

*"Town divided over Holt's death ... rumors spread that Sheriff Levi Powers held affections for Abigail Holt before her marriage. Sources claim she was seen arguing with him in his company weeks before her tragic passing."*

When we explored online sources, Lionel had offered his opinion about a potential link between the unscrupulous sheriff and Abigail Holt. Perhaps the sheriff forced unwanted advances on Abigail. The Gazette reporter back in his day also speculated on a romantic entanglement. I sat back in the hard wooden chair, the wheels of history turning in my mind. If Levi Powers had pursued Abigail ... and she died from a miscarriage, or worse, from Levi's own hand, then Silas had been nothing more than a scapegoat. Hanged to cover up the crime and preserve the reputation of the Powers name. Something to think about. I wondered who else would know the truth.

And now, generations later, Marlon Powers had met his end on that same elm. Justice delayed ... or a curse repeated? Had the Powers family male descendants been cursed?

I scribbled in my notebook; the pencil scratching fast.

#1 Silas Holt falsely accused ... Abigail possibly killed by Levi Powers
#2 Powers family gained land and influence after Holt's death
#3 Marlon, a descendant of Levi, repeats cruelty and control
#4 Margaret Quinton tied into town history by marriage and by Johnny Wiley? Or John Kelce?

The connections wound tight as garland on a Christmas tree. Every thread led back to that tree, that family, and the curse.

Luke would have wagged his tail at me for chasing shadows, but my gut told me it wasn't shadows at all. The truth waited, buried in brittle pages and fading ink.

I closed the Gazette volume with a soft thump. The room felt colder, as though unseen eyes still lingered in the corners of the archive. Grannie's voice whispered faintly at my shoulder …

*"You're close, Maddie girl. Don't stop now, keep your promise."*

I whispered back, "I will."

And with that, I packed my notes.

# Chapter Fourteen

## High School Memories

Setting out on foot after having returned the rental car, I left the newspaper office and headed down the street to the post office. Tall mounds of snow along the street, pushed high by the snowplows, created a wall around the sidewalk. The narrow path had been shoveled just wide enough for one person to pass. The sun shone brightly in the clear blue sky, but the wind carried a nip to it as I walked. Swirls of snowflakes spun in the air like miniature tornadoes where the wind whipped up the fluffy piles lying undisturbed on lawns or rooftops. I kept my head down against the chilly breeze, watching where I placed my feet, but not seeing ahead far enough to avoid bumping into someone trying to navigate the same narrow path.

"Oomph! Sorry!" I exclaimed as I plowed into a man bundled up in a heavy coat and knit scarf covering the lower half of his face.

We each reached out to steady the other to prevent ourselves from sitting in a snow pile. I raised my eyes to study the masked face and realized it was Joe Wiley.

"Miss Maddie, is that you? Are you all right? Goodness, I almost knocked you over," Joe said.

"No problem Joe. The fault is mine. I wasn't watching where I was going. Let's get up onto the steps and out of this wind," I said.

Joe backed up, and I followed him to the entrance of the post office, where the side of the building protected us from the blowing snow and frigid wind.

"Some storm we had, wasn't it? Heard you folks had some trouble at the inn. Everything okay now?" Joe asked.

"Yes, we're fine. You heard about Marlon Powers, then. Did you and your family have a nice Christmas?" I asked.

"Oh my, yes! Terrible thing about Marlon. I suppose that detective you're so fond of is on the case. My brother Johnny got home right before that blizzard hit and we all just hunkered down with a fire in that old potbelly stove and plenty of food. Had a really nice Christmas despite the storm."

"Where's your brother living these days? If memory serves me correctly, he's your older brother. Is that right?"

"No, Johnny is my younger brother. He's got a place over in Raleigh. Him and Adele, that's his wife, drove over on the twenty-second. They're hoping to head back home today or tomorrow if the roads are clear, that's why I'm out running errands and opening the store. Folks need bags of rock salt and shovels," Joe said with a muffled chuckle.

"Well, I'm glad you had a long visit with your brother. I think this storm took us all by surprise. Good seeing you, Joe. Y'all take care now," I said as I shook his gloved hand and then turned to dash up the steps and enter the post office.

Unlocking the inn's post office box, I pulled out the accumulated mail and did a quick sort. Numerous advertising flyers and junk mail got tossed into the trash can. I'd open the other mail and read it once I got back home. I tucked the envelopes into my bag and set off again.

My mind replayed the conversation I'd just had. So, Johnny Wiley had been in Clarkstown during the same time period that someone killed Marlon Powers. And Joe Wiley knew about the death. Interesting.

I hurried down the street and turned up the short alley leading over to Lily's office. The alley had not been shoveled, but I plunged ahead in knee-deep snow. Lights were on in the doctor's building. I could see a few people sitting in the waiting room as I passed under the windows. Tapping my boots against the side of the concrete steps, I knocked off the loose snow before entering the building. A man holding his hand wrapped in a towel glanced at me as I entered, then sat back and leaned his head against the wall behind him. A woman with a child on her lap looked my way but averted her tired eyes as I sat down and loosened my coat. The child appeared to be no more than four or five years old, with a flushed face and droopy eyes. He sucked his thumb as he cuddled against his mother's chest. One look at the patients waiting to see the doctor told me I'd have to wait my turn to speak with my friend. Their needs came first.

An elderly man shuffled out of the exam room and into the lobby, buttoning his coat and pulling down a wool cap over his ears. Behind him, a young woman in a nurse's uniform surveyed the occupants and then beckoned to the man with the wrapped hand.

"Mister Peters, the doctor can see you now."

He rose slowly, carefully cradling his hand, and followed the young nurse.

I shrugged out of my coat, picked up a *Country Home* magazine and prepared to wait. I was halfway through an article on refinishing antique furniture when Peters emerged with his hand and wrist bandaged and a look of relief on his face. The mother and child were next to see the doctor; I was glad no other patients had entered the office.

Tossing the magazine onto the table, I rose as Lily accompanied the woman into the lobby. Her eyes widened when she spotted me waiting.

"Now Missus Carter, be sure and give little Danny lots of water and fruit juices for the next day. Limit his milk intake to avoid creating extra phlegm for the time being. This medication should take effect in the next hour and the fever will go down. You call me if it doesn't or if he has any difficulty breathing." Lily handed the woman a small bag of sample pills and a written prescription.

"Thank you Doctor Chung. I feel much better now that you've seen Danny. The poor little tyke didn't have much of a Christmas what with being so sick."

"He'll be up and running around in a day or so."

"Thank you again. God bless you," the mother said.

Lily smiled as she saw them out and then turned to me.

"Don't tell me you're sick too," Lily said and waved me to follow her down the hall toward her private office.

"No, I'm okay. Just wanted to say hello while I was in town. Who's the new nurse? Looks like you've been busy. "

"I have. Typical head colds, some bronchitis, cuts, and bruises ... usual stuff. Betsy is helping out, earning extra credit in her nursing course at the medical center. What have you been up to?" Lily asked as she relaxed in her desk chair.

"I've been digging through old newspaper records and I'm headed to the library to check some high school yearbooks," I said.

"What are you looking for inside yearbooks?"

"Well, Margaret Powers told us her boyfriend was named Johnny. I've narrowed it down to two likely men ... Johnny Wiley or John Kelce. I wanted to check high school year books and see if I can find them and what years they graduated. Maybe it will help determine which one was the correct age to be seeing Margaret when she was sixteen."

"Wow! That's some sleuthing. What if they're both within her age range? How do you know they were in town during the past days and had the opportunity to do murder?"

"I just ran into Joe Wiley at the post office. His brother Johnny was home for Christmas. In fact, Joe made a point of telling me his brother came into town on the twenty-second and was supposed to leave today. So that definitely puts him in the region," I said.

"What about the other one, Kelce?" Lily asked.

"I don't know about him yet. I'm still gathering info."

"Okay, Nancy Drew, just don't go getting yourself into trouble while you're at it and stay warm out there. Just because the snow storm has passed doesn't mean those temperatures are warming up any. Be sure to bundle up and take care."

"Yes, doctor. I will. Promise." I smiled at my friend and gave her a quick hug, then wrapped up again under her watchful eye before heading out into the cold.

A short two-block walk found me at the Clarkstown Public Library. The small two-story building contained a small collection of local memorabilia and a rotating inventory of fiction and nonfiction books on loan from the larger county library system. I headed toward the local history department and found a bookcase filled with Clark-stown Panthers high school yearbooks. They were in numerical order by year. I ran my finger along the spines until I found books for 1998, 1999, 2000, 2001, and 2002. Since I didn't have any idea whether Margaret's boyfriend was young or older than her, I thought I'd scan a range of dates.

Opening the oldest book, 1998, I searched through the seniors' names listed alphabetically. No Kelce or Wiley. Moving on to the next book, 1999, I turned the pages of senior profiles and thrilled to see John Kelce among the seniors. His profile write-up described him as a handsome young man with a wicked sense of humor. He was a member of the football and wrestling teams.

Flipping through the pages to the end of the alphabet, I searched for Wiley but found none. I opened the next book and skimmed past the middle of the alphabet and went straight to the back. In 2001, John Wiley was a senior, and Margaret Quinton's picture was included among the junior girls crowned at the spring prom. So John Wiley would have been in school at the same time as Margaret, but John Kelce would have been three years ahead of her. I read the profile of John Wiley and learned he performed in the school play, was a member of the baseball team, and had been voted best dancer in his class.

Snapping pictures of both senior pages, I wasn't sure whether the information helped me to determine which man could have been Margaret's boyfriend and Claire's father. I didn't feel any closer than before.

"Maddie! Hello, Maddie," a voice called my name in a loud stage whisper.

I turned to see the source and found Amanda Fitzwilliams behind the checkout desk of the library. She smiled and waved enthusiastically as I neared the desk.

"I thought I recognized you. Hard to tell these days with everyone covered from head to toe. How are you dear?" asked Amanda.

"Just fine, thank you. How about yourself? What are you doing in the library?" I asked.

"Oh, I volunteer a few hours twice a week. You know, check out books and shelve returns. Nothing strenuous. Gives the librarian time to do her research projects and keep up with administrative duties."

"Well I'm sure the library appreciates your time and work," I said.

"Is it true about Marlon Powers?" asked Amanda. The twinkle in her eye showed her delight in hearing gossip firsthand and before Mildred Ginther.

"If you heard that Mister Powers died, then you heard correctly. How did you know?" I asked.

"Oh you know, small town and all that. News travels."

"Well, I can't say more than that; the investigation is still on going," I said in an appropriately stern voice that Allen would have approved.

"Oh dear! Poor Margaret. Whatever will she do with herself now? She must be sick with grief," Amanda said.

She paused as if she were waiting for me to interject more, and it made me think of Claire. Did Amanda expect me to comment on Margaret Powers reuniting with her daughter?

I glanced at my watch and the clock on the wall. "Is that the correct time? Good gracious, it's later than I thought. I really must be going. Nice seeing you again Amanda and Merry Christmas," I said. Pulling my cell phone from my purse, I dialed Sally back at the inn as I exited the library.

Sally picked up on the second ring. "Hey there. Need that ride home? I've been wondering when you'd call. I'll be about fifteen minutes. Where do you want me to meet you?"

"How about in the parking lot of the Piggly-Wiggly? I'll dash in and get some extra milk while I'm waiting on you," I said as I hiked down the snowy path toward the market.

"Okay. Be there as soon as I can," said Sally.

While I browsed through the market, I punched in Allen's number and felt pleased when he picked up on the second ring.

"Hey you. What's up?" he asked.

"I've got some information to show you. Can you come out to the house later? Tom's pecan pie is still waiting to be cut, if that's any incentive to you."

"Ah, that is tempting. What time do you want me there?"

"How about six or six-thirty? I'll see about fixing us a light supper," I said.

"Perfect," Allen said with a smile in his voice. Things were beginning to look up. Mmm ... pecan pie and a pretty gal.

# Chapter Fifteen

## Old Friends

Sally added napkins to the place settings on the sturdy kitchen table. She breathed in the aroma of the beef pot roast simmering on the stove.

"Hope you don't mind my fixing the roast for dinner. It seemed like the simplest thing to cook for the two of us; just throw all the ingredients in the Dutch oven and let it simmer for hours until it's tender and we're ready to eat."

"Are you kidding? This is perfect and it smells delicious. I, uh, invited Detective Crawford for dinner too. We've got some information to share and I thought it would be simpler if he came out to the house. I'll add another place setting to the table. He won't mind eating in the kitchen with us," I said.

"Okay. It's all right; he seems like a nice man. I'll always remember his kindness to me after that tunnel incident," Sally said, referring to the time thieves searching for gold coins had tied her up in a hidden tunnel. The near-death experience had traumatized Sally.

"Have you heard from Tom?" I asked as I sliced the loaf of French bread I had bought at the store.

"Mm-hmm. He called earlier while you were out. Said the heavy snow damaged the roof on his garden shed, caved it in, I guess. He was making repairs and if we didn't need him here, he'd be staying at home for the next day or so. I told him we were okay and getting along just fine," Sally said.

The crunch of tires on packed snow and the thrum of a car engine drew me to the kitchen window. I looked out to see Allen pulling in. He came onto the back porch, stomped the snow off his boots, and rapped on the door.

"Hi! C'mon in, you can hang up your coat and leave your boots in the mud room. Sally and I have dinner all ready. Hope you're hungry," I said.

Allen shrugged out of his heavy coat and shucked his boots as requested, then padded into the warm kitchen. Luke immediately barked on seeing him and butted his large head against Allen's leg, expecting the token scratch to his ears and jowls. Allen dutifully complied.

"Hey boy, how are you?" Allen asked the big shepherd as the two nuzzled, both giving and receiving attention.

"Sally made a pot roast, complete with potatoes and carrots cooked in the beef broth. She deserves all the credit for tonight's meal. All I contributed was the loaf of bread. Go wash your hands and sit over here," I said, pointing to the chair at the head of the table.

Opening a bottle of red wine, I poured three glasses and then set the bottle in the center of the table next to the bread basket and butter dish.

Sally spooned out a healthy portion of tender beef and vegetables onto each plate and then joined us at the table. It was a tasty meal that stuck to your ribs on a wintry day.

"Mmm, this is really good. Thanks for inviting me. I've certainly had my share of delicious meals here this week. I won't know how to pay you back for your hospitality."

"That's what I do ... hospitality, the essence of any bed and breakfast inn. You're always welcome," I said with a smile.

We all ate, enjoying the beef, and making small conversation about the weather. When Sally rose to start a pot of coffee and bring out the pecan pie for dessert, Allen turned to me expectantly.

"So what have you been investigating that you wanted to share with me?" he asked.

"I've been reading more of Sara Brooke's journals for one thing. If you recall, I did promise to learn more about the death of Abigail Holt and Silas' trial. Sara wrote she believed Levi Powers killed Abigail in a fit of rage. He had been pursuing Abigail and she had rejected his attentions. It's all there in Sara's diary. Oh yes, I also spent several hours going through newspaper files down at the Gazette. There was a reporter who also wrote an article questioning the death of Abigail and the subsequent hanging. So that's two accounts."

"Okay. That's interesting. How does that information impact our current murder case?" Allen asked. He sat back and sipped his wine.

"Well, it probably doesn't, but like I said ... I promised I'd look into it. But you know, Lionel had researched the Powers' family tree online while he was here and we found it incredibly interesting that all the men in the Powers family died in their mid-forties after 1902. Isn't that odd? Not a one of them lived to reach fifty years old. Some died of heart attacks, illness, others in an accident of some type. All the Powers men died at about the same age as Silas Holt. Weird! Right?" I asked as I savored that bit of historical information.

"What are you saying? That Silas Holt cursed the Powers family or caused the death of the male heirs?"

"Maybe. Something like that. If he didn't, then why is it that all the records show the Powers' ancestors before 1902 living to be a ripe old age into their seventies or eighties? I just don't think it should be dismissed," I said.

"All right. You found out all that history today, huh?"

"Mm-hmm and more. I also read about the society wedding of Marlon Powers and Margaret Quinton in March of 2002. It was big to-do. Remember Margaret telling us about her boyfriend Johnny and that he was Claire's father? So, I got to thinking ... how many men named John or Johnny would have been in Clarkstown and close to her age at that time? We know her wedding date and we know Claire's birthday, so if you count back nine months or so, that's got to be when Margaret spent time with her Johnny. I found two prospective candidates," I said.

"You got all this from a newspaper clipping? Are you going to tell me the last names?" Allen asked, sitting forward, with a spark of interest in his eyes.

"That plus the high school yearbooks. I found Johnny Wiley in the class of 2001 and John Kelce in the class of 1999. Either or both men would have known Margaret when she was in high school. Check out their senior profile pages from the yearbooks. I grabbed a photo of each one," I said, handing Allen my cell phone and bringing up the pictures.

"Okay, so you think you've narrowed down her boyfriend to one of these men. Doesn't mean either of them had opportunity or motive to kill Marlon Powers at Christmas time."

"According to Joe Wiley, his brother was in town visiting during the holiday, from the twenty-third until today. That gives him opportunity. I haven't had a chance to speak to Jeb Kelce about his brother, but I can ask him when I return old Painter. That will give me a legitimate excuse to stop in," I said. A plan was forming in my mind, and I knew I had to carry it out.

"I'm not sure I like the idea of you poking your nose into a possibly dangerous situation. Maybe I should go with you."

"It doesn't take two people to walk a horse back home. Don't be silly. I'll be perfectly safe."

"Nevertheless, I think I'll tag along."

"Okay, if you insist, but it's too dark to return Painter tonight. I'll have to do it tomorrow. Did you want to come back or, um, spend the night?" I asked, suddenly embarrassed at being so forward with the man.

Allen raised his eyebrows at my suggestion, then gave a light cough into his hand. "I think perhaps it would be better if I returned in the morning. Besides, I don't have a change of clothes to allow me to spend the night."

My feelings bordered on disappointment and relief.

"Can you run a background check on both men?"

"I'll look into their current status, but technically, I can't run a background check on an individual without them being a suspect and what you've given me is pretty slim. Just conjecture at this point. Sorry Maddie."

"That's disappointing, but I guess I understand. Still, we need to learn where both of these guys were the day Powers died, storm or no storm. I've got a niggling hunch I can't dismiss."

We took our cups of coffee into the living room and settled near the crackling fire in the hearth. The twinkle lights on the Christmas tree winked, and the cozy room still carried a light fragrance from the fresh fir and pine. I took a deep breath as the serene scene calmed my earlier qualms.

"Give me a stronger motive and I'll consider your boyfriend idea as a reasonable suspect. Maybe we can learn more tomorrow," Allen said as we cuddled together.

# Chapter Sixteen

## Horse Sense

It was mid-morning when I led old Painter up the frozen lane to the Kelce farm a mile away with Allen walking beside me, his collar turned up against the cold. I wore my heavy hiking boots again along with flannel-lined corduroy slacks, an Irish wool sweater and my heaviest down-filled parka. The cold air still nipped at my cheeks and nose, giving me a rosy look.

I held the horse's reins in my mittened hands, coaxing him along beside me. The gelding's hooves crunched in the thin crust of snow, and every puff of his breath came out white as pipe smoke. The Kelce place sat low against the hills; its barns and outbuildings hunkered down in weathered gray boards. A strip of smoke curled lazily from the chimney, smelling of hickory wood.

Jeb Kelce stepped out of the barn before we even reached the gate. His shoulders were stooped, but his eyes darted, quick as a crow's. He peered at me, then at Allen, then at Painter.

"Brought your horse back," I called, patting Painter's shaggy neck. "Don't know how he got out, but he weathered the storm in our barn okay. Tom fed him some hay."

Jeb gave a grunt and came forward to take the reins. "Lucky he didn't break a leg on that road ice. He's too old for such foolish riding."

Allen spoke before I could answer. "Funny thing, Jeb. Painter showed up over at Magnolia Blossom Inn the night of the blizzard. Not every horse would've found his way through those drifts."

The farmer's mouth tightened. "Guess he still remembers the trail. He's been around here long enough."

I let my mittened hand slide down Painter's mane, then said lightly, "There was a lot of commotion at the inn that night ... Christmas Eve. You must have heard about it. Baby born, a tree hit by lightning, and Marlon Powers found dead."

Jeb's gaze flicked to mine ... just for a heartbeat, but enough. He tugged at the bit, keeping his eyes on the horse instead of me. "Small town. Yeah, word travels."

"Did you know Margaret or Marlon Powers?" I asked, keeping my tone casual but watching him closely.

Jeb's jaw worked. "Everybody knew Margaret. Pretty girl, smart, shy but uppity. John liked her once. But that was years back."

"So your brother John," Allen prodded, "when did he leave Clarkstown? Was that in 2001?"

"Might be. Went north to find work," Jeb said quickly. "Didn't suit him to farm."

"How is your brother? Did you get to enjoy a family Christmas?" I asked.

I heard the hesitation ... that brief pause before he added, "He came home for Christmas, stayed three days, then headed back. Lives in Crozet now. Runs a garage there."

"That must have been nice for you. Family is everything," I said. "You know, I saw John's name in a high school yearbook recently. I didn't know he was on the football and wrestling teams. Bet he was popular among the girls in school. Did he date Margaret back in the day?" I asked and watched his face flush. His hand snaked to rub the back of his neck.

"High school is ancient history. What does John's dating choices have to do with anything?" Jeb demanded in a harsh voice.

Allen crossed his arms, his breath steaming in the cold. "Convenient timing, that's all. Margaret went away to Atlanta during 2001, same year John went north, wasn't it?"

Jeb's eyes flicked to Allen, hard as flint. "I don't keep track of Margaret Quinton. She made her choices. So did John. His private life is his own. You'll have to question him."

The silence that followed was sharp enough to cut with a knife. I let it hang there, then glanced toward the barn behind him. A darker shape moved inside, the shuffle of hooves against straw.

"Painter has company in there," I said, narrowing my eyes. "You've another horse stabled. How do you think Painter got loose?"

Jeb shifted his weight. "That's John's mare. He leaves her here to ride when he's in town."

I noticed he avoided my other question about how Painter got out.

My pulse picked up. If John had a horse stabled here, he could have followed whoever had stolen Painter through the snowstorm. The blowing snow rapidly covered the horse's tracks. Assuming Marlon used the horse to get to the inn after his car slid off the road, John could have tracked him.

Allen's gaze met mine for a brief second, and I knew he was thinking the same thing.

I reached out to scratch Painter's nose. "Well, glad we could shelter your horse during that storm and he's all right. No harm done, it would appear."

Jeb nodded curtly, already leading the gelding away toward the barn. His boots crunched hard in the snow, and I couldn't shake the sense that he was glad to see our backs.

Allen and I held hands as we trudged down the snowy road back to the inn. A hot cup of coffee would be a welcome sight about now. My hands felt frozen within my woolen mittens. I looked forward to wrapping them around a steaming mug.

As Allen and I walked down the lane, he muttered under his breath, "That man's hiding something. And if John Kelce's horse was in that barn the entire storm ... then who was really riding Painter through the drifts?"

"Got to be Marlon Powers. I don't see any other answer."

I pulled my scarf tighter, heart thudding. "Either Jeb's lying about his brother's coming and going during Christmas ... or someone else used that horse to follow Marlon Powers that night."

"You're probably right, but Powers made other enemies that might have taken advantage of the storm to mask their activities. I can't discount them just yet," Allen said as he pulled open the kitchen door and we staggered into its warmth. After a hot coffee and something to eat, we'd be ready to go again.

"Refresh my memory, why are we stopping at the Legion post?" Allen asked as he parked his car in the lot.

"Two reasons. I really want to buy some tickets for the New Year's Eve party for all of us and I heard Marlon Powers spent a lot of time hanging out here with his buddies. Maybe you can learn something."

The American Legion post sat low and square at the edge of town, its flag whipping in the stiff wind that still carried the bite of the storm. Allen held the post door for me, and a wash of warm air rolled out, laced with the smells of fried chicken wings, beer, and cigarette smoke that had seeped into the wood walls over decades.

A string of silver tinsel garland drooped over the bar, and a crooked paper Santa grinned down at us. A small artificial tree stood in the corner. It was covered with plastic and glass ornaments from around the globe, donated by legion members.

I tugged off my gloves and rubbed my hands together. "I just want to check the time for the New Year's Eve party," I told Allen, glancing at the flyers tacked to the cork board near the door.

"You're determined to drag me out in a suit and tie," Allen teased me.

"You say that like it's punishment," I said, brushing snow off my coat. "What better way to shake off this Christmas chaos than dancing into the new year?"

Allen gave me a faint smile, but I could see the crease between his brows hadn't eased since the discovery of Marlon Powers' body. He had detective work written all over his face, even here.

The place was quiet this time of day … three men bent over a pool table, the sharp click of balls echoing in the room; another sat at the bar nursing a highball, his elbows planted wide.

Behind the bar, Hank, the grizzled bartender, was polishing glasses with a rag that had seen better days. "Detective Crawford," he greeted Allen, then looked at me. "Maddie Brooke, lovely as usual. Looking for party tickets? They're going quick."

"Yes," I said, leaning on the bar. "I've got a whole group who wants to come … if we're not too late. What time does the New Year's Eve party start?"

"Nine o'clock, band starts at ten," Hank said. "Always a fun time: raffles, dancing, a midnight champagne toast."

"Great. I need six tickets. We'll want our own table."

Hank handed me a strip of tickets as I slid the money to him across the bar. He poured a draft beer for Allen and a Coke for me, then ran a bar towel across the wooden surface.

Allen stepped up to the bar. "Have you seen Marlon Powers in here recently? I understand this is his favorite watering hole." He sipped his beer as he studied the bartender's face.

"Yeah, he was in here the afternoon of the twenty-third. Gets together with old Army buddies. But on that day, he drank more whiskey than common sense allowed. Never saw him act that way. I mean, the man has a temper and everyone knows it, but he was fit to be tied. Like he'd been stewing on something for years and it had just erupted. Caused a bit of a stir. I haven't seen him since, but then, we were closed due to the blizzard and for Christmas day."

Allen straightened. "Tell me about this stir he made."

Hank set down the glass. His voice dropped, meant only for us. "Marlon was slurring, pounding the bar with his fist. Kept growling that his wife made a mistake years back, and he was the only one left to clean it up. Said he should've done it long ago. He couldn't forgive her. Had to protect his reputation. Scared a couple of the older vets clean off their stools."

A chill prickled along my arms. I could picture Marlon red-faced, eyes wild, the smell of liquor on his breath. "Who was here?" I asked, my voice tighter than I meant.

Hank ticked names off on his fingers. "John Wiley, sat by the jukebox with his brother Joe. John Kelce sat at the far table, playing poker with Pete Hollis and Carl Minton. And Sam Riggs was here too ... he's done business with Powers for years. The whole place heard him cursing, no doubt about that. Sam tried to settle him down but Powers threw a punch at him so he backed off. Place went quiet when he started a fight."

Hank scrubbed the bar top again, his voice lowering. "He didn't say Margaret by name. But we knew who he meant. Men here can count, we're not dumb. We remember when Margaret Quinton left town then came back ten months later to marry Marlon Powers. Talk of that girl, Claire, had been buzzing around town all day before

Marlon came in. Marlon called her a 'mistake that should've stayed buried.' Real ugly talk."

Allen's mouth set in a grim line. "And when he left?"

"Stumbled out into the cold like a man looking for a fight," Hank said. "Could hardly stand straight, but he had that murderous look in his eye."

"Anyone else leave with Powers?" asked Allen.

"Both Kelce and Wiley ran out after him. Marlon didn't say where he was going. He jumped in his car and took off before any of us could take his keys away. I don't like guys driving drunk; you gotta believe that I don't sanction that."

Allen nodded and then tugged on my hand. I tucked the slip of tickets into my purse, but my mind was far from midnight champagne. Outside, the wind whipped against my cheeks, and Allen's stride was long and fast.

We sat in the parked car mulling over the bartender's words. Allen started the engine, and warm air flowed onto us.

"What do you think? I can see the wheels turning in that pretty head of yours," Allen said.

"Allen," I said breathlessly, "if Marlon left drunk, ranting, and both Johns heard him ... doesn't it make sense one of them followed him? Maybe even confronted him?"

Allen clenched his jaw. "It makes sense. Too much sense. But the trouble is ... which John? Or both?"

My stomach turned. I thought of Margaret's face, of Claire's pale, stricken look when she shut herself away upstairs. Was Claire the mistake Marlon raged about? Was she the secret he thought needed *taken care of,* and would Margaret do anything to protect her child?

And then another thought struck me like a gust of icy wind.

"Claire had been all over town asking questions, hinting at a search for her birth mother. We know for certain that Margaret and

Marlon both heard her and realized her identity. What if others heard her? If both Johns were here," I said slowly, "then both of them might've heard exactly what Marlon meant. They would have put two and two together and guessed Claire was the mistake Margaret had made. "

Allen's eyes locked on mine. "Then one of them might have followed him. Hank said they both left at the same time."

"Out of anger? Or sense of paternity?" My voice quavered before I steadied it. "Think of it, Allen. What if one of them realized Claire was his daughter ... the daughter he never knew existed? And after years of silence, after town gossip stirred everything up, he confirms the truth right there in this bar? He'd want to protect her at any cost, wouldn't he?"

The air felt heavy in my chest. I could see it in my mind ... the bar going silent, the murmurs afterward, the growing questions, and Marlon's ugly muttering.

"And if one of them believed Marlon had ruined their chance to know their own daughter.... That might have been enough to push a man over the edge," Allen said, finishing my thoughts.

Allen's brows drew together. Finally, he decided, "I need to talk to both Wiley and Kelce. Separately, without family protecting them. See which one slips. Let's get you home. Lucas and I need to make some calls."

I nodded, though my heart felt tangled in knots. "If Marlon's death was no accident that night, then maybe his death wasn't just about Margaret or his business dealings. Maybe it was about blood. About family. About a father's instincts to protect his daughter from harm."

And I couldn't shake the sense that whichever John it was, he might still be out there ... angry, afraid, and holding more secrets than he knew what to do with.

# Chapter Seventeen

## Alibis

The drive to Crozet took them along back roads still rimmed with snow, the hills gleaming pale blue in the morning sun. Salt crust crunched beneath the tires of Lucas's cruiser, and each gust of wind whipped powdered snow into ghostly shapes along the fencerows.

John Kelce's garage sat on the edge of town, a long, low building with a corrugated tin roof and the sour, oily tang of motor grease thick in the air. A battered Chevy pickup stood in the lot, its tailgate bent from years of hard use.

Allen and Lucas stepped inside, boots echoing on the concrete floor. The place was warmer than expected; an old propane heater rattled in the corner, but the air carried the pungent smells of gasoline, rubber, and sweat. John Kelce straightened from under the hood of a Buick, wiping his hands on a rag that was already blackened.

He was leaner and younger-looking than Allen had imagined, but with lines etched deep into his sun-weathered face. His eyes narrowed when he saw the detectives, though his shoulders didn't stiffen in surprise.

"Detective Crawford," Kelce said. "And you must be Wampler. Heard you two were sniffin' around after that business up Clarkstown way. Jeb said he thought you'd be by."

"So you aren't surprised to see us," Allen said.

Lucas flashed his badge. "We're following up, Mr. Kelce. We'd like to ask you some questions about the night of December twenty-third."

Kelce smirked without humor. "That'd be the night Marlon Powers stumbled into Jeb's barn like a fool." He tossed the rag aside. "Yeah, I figured you were comin'."

Allen's tone remained clipped, professional. "Let's start at the Legion that afternoon. Tell us what you recall. You must have witnessed Powers drinking, heard him ranting about his wife's mistake."

Kelce shrugged. "Whole bar heard it. He was sloppier than usual, mean drunk. I didn't want to tangle with him there, so I let him go."

"Tangle with him. Were you planning on tangling with him, as you say?" Allen asked. His eyes narrowed as he studied the man.

Lucas leaned forward slightly. "You let him go ... but you followed him, didn't you?"

A flicker crossed Kelce's face ... reluctance, maybe shame, but then he gave a curt nod. "Yeah. Man could barely walk straight. He drove that big Lincoln of his right into a drift on the county road near Jeb's place. Stupid fool couldn't get it out of the ditch. I went ahead and pulled into my brother's garage. Next thing I know, Powers is staggering into my Jeb's barn and untying old Painter like it was his God-given right."

Allen caught the faint tremor in his voice, though Kelce covered it with a rough laugh.

"You confronted him?" Allen asked.

Kelce's jaw worked. "Damn right I did. Told him to leave the horse. He was out of his head, raving about needing to get to some girl, about fixing a mistake. Powers jumped onto old Painter and gave him a kick in the side, leaping out of the barn. Headed off down the road. I swung onto my mare and took off after him."

The heater hissed in the corner. For a moment, the only sound in the garage was the ticking of cooling metal under the Buick's hood.

Lucas said in a low voice, "And then?"

"I caught up with him at the Brooke's barn. He was hell bent on making trouble and I was just as determined that he wouldn't. We got into it ... he swung at me, missed. I laid him out with a single punch."

"What was so important that you had to stop Powers? Was it Claire? Your daughter?" Lucas asked.

John Kelce sucked in his breath. "You leave her out of it."

"Did you hit him in the head with a heavy object?" Allen asked.

"No. Just my fist. I dragged him to a hay pile. He was breathing. Out cold but breathing." Kelce's eyes flicked to the detectives. "Tied Painter in the stall, he was breathing hard and I couldn't handle leading two horses in that strong wind. I mounted my mare, and rode back to the farm before the blizzard closed the roads. I swear I left Powers in one piece. Alive."

Allen studied him. The man's story was too detailed to be fabricated on the spot. Still ... there were gaps. "When you left him, did anyone else see you? Anyone who can confirm you went home and stayed there?"

Kelce hesitated, then shook his head. "No. Nobody at the inn saw me, at least I don't think so. I went back to Jeb's so we could spend Christmas together. Electric went out in the storm. It was just the two of us. Only thing I can swear is what I did ... and didn't do. I didn't kill Marlon Powers."

The smell of motor oil pressed heavy around them, the heater popping sporadically. Allen glanced at Lucas, who had his notebook open, pen hovering.

Lucas asked, "You admit to assault. You admit you left him unconscious. What if he never woke up?"

Kelce's voice hardened. "He woke up. He had to. I didn't hit him that hard. Someone else got to him after I left. You boys know it as well as I do."

Allen's eyes narrowed. "That still leaves us with one question: if it wasn't you, Mr. Kelce ... who finished him off?"

Kelce didn't answer. He simply reached for his rag again, wiping hands that were already clean, his silence louder than any denial. He refused to say more or meet their eyes.

When they left the garage, Lucas exhaled a low whistle, the cold air biting his breath into vapor. "Well. He gave us enough to arrest him for assault, but not for murder."

Allen pulled his coat collar up, his gaze on the snow-capped ridges beyond town. "No. He's not lying about leaving Powers alive. But I think he's leaving something out. Like Claire. I could feel it. Which means someone else made the final blow and put that rope around his neck ... someone we haven't pinned down yet. We may have to speak to Mr. Kelce again."

The wind whistled over the tin roof as if to underline the words. Somewhere in the puzzle of Clarkstown's history and family secrets, the fatal blow to Marlon Powers still waited to be uncovered.

By mid-afternoon, the snow along Charlottesville's streets had turned gray and slushy, plows finally making headway against the drifts. Inside the precinct, Allen and Lucas sat in the cramped interview room, the hum of the overhead fluorescent light buzzing dimly above them. The forensics report lay open on the table between them, its stark language offering no comfort.

**Cause of death:** blunt force trauma to the back of the skull.

**Likely weapon:** iron lantern recovered near barn door. Trace of lamp oil in wound.

**Manner of hanging:** staged postmortem.

Allen rubbed his chin. "So Kelce's punch didn't kill him. The lantern did."

Lucas nodded grimly. "Which begs the question ... who picked it up and swung it? And why string him up in that tree?"

Their next stop was back in Clarkstown at Joe Wiley's neat brick colonial. Holiday lights still twinkled along the gutters, though the wreath on the door hung slightly askew, weather beaten after days of wind and snow. Joe answered, his heavyset frame filling the doorway, the scent of pine and roast beef drifting from inside.

"Detectives," he said warily. "Come on in."

Inside, they found John Wiley by the fireplace, his Marine haircut long since grown out but his posture still straight-backed. He rose to shake Allen's hand firmly. His wife Adele sat close by, knitting needles clicking in steady rhythm, her watchful eyes never leaving the men.

Allen wasted no time. "Mr. Wiley, we're confirming your whereabouts on December twenty-third and twenty-forth."

Wiley's voice was calm, almost clipped. "I was here, at my brother's. Snow made travel impossible. Adele and I drove up from Raleigh on the twenty-second to spend Christmas with Joe and his family. We never left this house after the storm came down. You can ask anyone in town ... we were seen at church on the twenty-third, then we hunkered down here."

Joe backed him up, arms folded. "He never left. Roads were shut. You know that as well as I do."

Lucas studied Wiley, his tone careful. "You were at the Legion on the twenty-third when Powers caused a scene."

Wiley's jaw tightened. "Yes, right before the storm got bad. I heard every word he said about his wife. About some mistake. A man oughtn't to speak about his wife like that. But if you're asking, no, I didn't follow him. I had no interest in his business, then or now."

Adele's needles stilled. "John had nothing to do with that mess, Detective. We had planned on leaving for home today, but John said we should stay until he spoke with you."

Allen and Lucas exchanged a glance. Wiley's alibi—two families vouching for him, snowbound together—was solid. No way he slipped out, not with the drifts swallowing cars whole that night. Joe Wiley's house was on the other side of town and several miles from Maddie's inn, difficult to get there, kill Powers and return home without being missed.

Later, back at the precinct, they turned their attention to Sam Riggs. Unlike Wiley, Riggs had no polished manners. He arrived in a grease-stained coat, with the sharp scent of tobacco clinging to him, his eyes restless. His feet dragged as he entered the station on the arm of a patrolman.

Allen nodded to the officer as Riggs reluctantly slid into a chair.

"Thanks, officer. We'll take it from here," Allen said.

Lucas slid the forensics photo across the table, the iron lantern circled in red. "You were at the Legion on the twenty-third, Mr. Riggs. You heard Powers threatening to 'fix' his wife's mistake. I understand he took a swing at you."

Riggs shifted uncomfortably. "I heard him, yeah. He was drunker than a skunk, carrying on like always. I figured it was just bluster."

Allen leaned in. "You've done business with Powers. You knew him better than most."

A bitter laugh escaped Riggs. "Business? More like he bled me dry. He promised land deals, contracts that never came through. Left me holding debts I still haven't crawled out of. Man was poison."

Lucas's voice was even. "Sounds like motive, Mr. Riggs."

Riggs slammed his hand on the table, the sound sharp in the small room. "Motive, maybe. Opportunity, no. When the storm hit, I was stuck at my sister's farm twenty miles south. Roads were closed. I couldn't have been at that inn even if I wanted to."

Allen's eyes narrowed. "And can anyone confirm that?"

"My sister, her husband, half their neighbors. We spent Christmas Eve digging out their driveway and trying to keep the pipes from freezing. I never laid eyes on Powers again after the Legion."

They left Riggs seething, his resentment obvious, but his alibi as strong as Wiley's.

Back at their desks, Allen and Lucas reviewed the board. Wiley—alibied by family. Riggs—alibied by the storm. Kelce—admitted to the assault but swore Powers was alive when he left him in the barn. Margaret—arrived after the fact, though her motives were tangled in secrecy. Claire—too frightened, too unsteady, but undeniably linked to the case.

Allen tapped the forensics report again. "The lantern killed him. But who swung it? Everyone with a motive was either snowed in or accounted for. That just leaves the folks staying at the inn, us included."

Lucas exhaled slowly. "Which leaves us with the possibility we can't write on any report."

Allen's gaze lifted, weary but sharp. "The ghost."

Neither said it out loud, but both felt the unease settling over them. Someone, living or dead, had put Marlon Powers in that tree, and the list of suspects was shrinking to nothing.

# Chapter Eighteen

## History

The parlor of Amanda Fitzwilliams smelled faintly of lemon polish and rose sachet, the kind of scent that clung to the lace curtains and upholstered chairs like old secrets. Mildred Ginther sat straight-backed on the settee, her cane propped beside her, while Amanda fluttered about pouring tea with a precision that suggested she'd been preparing for this kind of visit for years. Amanda opened the box of Tom's special Christmas sugar cookies I had brought as a treat for the dear soul. She smiled at me as she arranged them on a Santa plate.

I opened my notebook, the pen poised, though I had a feeling most of what they'd tell me would linger in my head without ink.

"Thank you both for agreeing to meet me today. And thank you Miss Amanda for hosting. This may sound crazy, but I'm looking into the 1900 feud between Levi Powers and Silas Holt," I began. "My grandmother used to hint at it, but she didn't know the full story. All Grannie knew were the stories from Sara Brooke who was a midwife back then. Sara was my Grandpa Charles' grandmother. I've been reading some of her diaries. I thought you two might have heard more about the feud from your own families."

Mildred sniffed, eyes narrowing like a crow sighting something shiny. "Heard it? Honey, we were raised on it. My grandmother swore Levi Powers was the most dangerous man to ever wear a sheriff's badge. Didn't matter that the town thought he was a hero."

Amanda set the teapot down with a tiny clink. "Hero ... villain ... sometimes it's a matter of who tells the tale. My grandmother claimed Levi had his eye on Abigail Holt long before Silas came along. Said he courted her, if you can call it that. Abigail turned him away, married Silas, and that was the beginning of the bad blood. When a Powers wants something, they usually get it. The family has had this town under their thumb for decades."

I leaned forward. "Some records say Abigail died suddenly ... some whisper miscarriage, others something darker. Did either of your grandmothers say what really happened?"

Amanda hesitated, her hands fussing with the sugar bowl. "There were whispers she took a fall and hit her head, but Mildred's right, Levi had a temper. When she died, people said it wasn't an accident at all."

"I read one account of her death in the Gazette," I said.

Mildred's voice dropped, gravelly and sharp. "And when the mob hanged Silas ... led by Sheriff Powers himself ... well, folks figured Levi got rid of them both. Abigail gone, Silas disgraced, and Levi standing tall like justice had been served. Only... it was never justice. It was jealousy."

A shiver ran through me, not from the draft slipping through old windowpanes but from the way their words stitched together with what I already knew. History wasn't just old stories ... it was shadows stretching straight into the present.

"Maddie dear, why are you interested in that old story? Such a tragedy but it happened over a hundred years ago," Amanda said.

I closed my notebook deliberately. "I need to tell you something ... only a select few people know this and I trust it won't go any further than this drawing room. Marlon Powers wasn't just found dead in my barn. He was hanged in a tree ... the same elm tree used with Silas Holt over a hundred years ago."

Amanda gasped, one hand flying to her throat. "Oh my Lord! And it happened on Christmas Eve?"

Mildred's eyes sharpened, with a gleam of vindication there.

"You see, Amanda," she said, "it always comes back around. The Powers men, the Holt men ... that tree's cursed with their pride and their sins."

"I don't think it's the tree that's cursed, Mildred. Remember that old tale about Silas cursing the entire Powers family? You think back to all the men over the generations and how young they died. There's a curse working, but it's not in the tree," Amanda said in a firm voice, daring her friend to deny her reasoning.

I sat back, my heart thudding. Allen and Lucas were out chasing down suspects and piecing together alibis. I was here, listening to century-old gossip that sounded more like prophecy. And somewhere between the past and the present, between Levi Powers' vengeance and Marlon Powers' threats, the truth was waiting ... dark, tangled, and far closer than I liked.

By the time I left Amanda's parlor, the air outside felt sharper, like the cold had teeth. Heavy gray clouds hid what little sun that shone in the late afternoon sky. I pulled my coat tight, my mind buzzing louder than the wind rattling the shutters. Levi Powers, Abigail Holt, Silas Holt ... and now Marlon strung up like some macabre echo from the past. Coincidence? No. The story the women told me had too much weight, too much unfinished anger clinging to it.

Driving into Charlottesville, I needed to compare notes with Allen. I found a place to park a block from the police station and walked at a rapid pace from my car to the tall building, grateful to get out of the chilly wind blowing down the street.

I found Allen in his office, his desk buried under files and the glow of a desk lamp that made his face look more drawn than usual. Lucas had left already, but the faint smell of coffee told me they'd been grinding at the case hard.

"You look like you've dug up something," Allen said, glancing up at me.

"You don't know the half of it," I replied, shutting the door behind me. "I just came from Amanda Fitzwilliams' house. Mildred Ginther was there too."

His eyebrows lifted. "Town historians, if you can call them that."

"Town gossips," I corrected, "but sometimes gossip is just history that hasn't been dusted off. They told me their grandmothers swore Levi Powers had been after Abigail Holt long before she married Silas. When she died ... well, it wasn't a miscarriage or a fall. They think Levi had a hand in it. He shifted the evidence and blame onto Silas. And then when Silas was hanged in 1902, it was Levi leading the mob."

Allen leaned back in his chair, folding his arms. "And you think this has something to do with Marlon?"

I took a breath. "I know it does. Because Marlon was hanged in the elm tree, just like Silas Holt. You and I both witnessed it."

For the first time in days, I saw Allen's composure crack. His jaw clenched, and he sat forward, voice low. "We aren't releasing that detail to the public."

"I know," I said, meeting his gaze. "But it's the truth. And the parallels are too close to ignore. Whoever did this ... maybe they were making a statement. Maybe they were tying Marlon back to the sins of his own ancestors."

He rubbed a hand across his mouth, thinking. "We've focused on opportunity and alibis. But if you're right, there's a motive rooted deeper than just business disputes or jealous lovers."

"Exactly," I said, my pulse quickening. "What if someone believes Marlon carried the curse of Levi Powers ... that the Powers men always take what isn't theirs? Maybe they thought ending Marlon the way Silas ended was some kind of justice."

Allen was silent for a long moment. Then he pushed back his chair and stood. "I need to loop Lucas in. If this is more than coincidence, we're looking at a killer who isn't just hiding in the present ... they're reenacting history."

"And history," I said softly, "has a nasty habit of repeating itself."

Allen gave me a long look, the kind that said he wasn't sure whether to thank me or warn me off. But I could tell that, just like me, he felt the ground shifting. What had seemed like scattered pieces were aligning, and the picture they made wasn't pretty.

I sipped my coffee, pushing my empty plate to the side. Allen and I had grabbed a quick supper at Josie's diner near the campus. I'd forgotten how tasty the food was in the diner; it had been a couple of years since I'd eaten there when I attended UVA. Although my appetite was sated, my mind still hungered for an answer.

"When you spoke to John Kelce, did you get the impression that he knew about Claire being his daughter? I keep thinking of the scene described in the Legion and why he would have followed Marlon Powers in a snow storm. It certainly wasn't because he was concerned for his safety," I said with a snort. "You said John Wiley told you he went to Joe's house and didn't worry about Marlon's destination. And the same was true for his business acquaintance,

Sam Rigg. Right? So why did John Kelce track Marlon Powers to the inn?"

"Good question. I got the impression that he wasn't telling me the whole truth and I have to agree that the part he left out must be Claire," Allen said in a low voice for my ears only.

He glanced around the diner; it was starting to fill up. Standing up, he took the bill over to the cashier by the entrance and paid for our food.

Zipping my parka closed, I pulled my knit hat down over my ears and grabbed my gloves and then joined him near the door.

"I'm ready. Let's go."

Allen stared at me, then chuckled. "You know we're not walking. We can take the car and it has a heater and everything. You look like your ready for the ski slopes in that outfit."

"I get cold easily. Just because it's not snowing any more doesn't mean that wind won't whip right through you," I said, scuffing my boot against the doorframe. Just as we opened the door to exit the diner, a gust of wind ripped the door handle out of my hand and blasted us in the face. I shot Allen an *'I told you so'* look.

Allen opened his car door for me as I climbed in. I heard him mumble under his breath, "I stand corrected."

I couldn't help but grin. Not another peep from me; Mother Nature had said it all.

"What do you think, Lionel? Will the Gazette editor publish my piece? It's more than just a rehash of a murder trial from years ago. I think the residents of Clarkstown need to know the facts and settle the misinformed gossip that has spread over the decades."

I busied myself pouring cups of Earl Grey tea and serving slices of the remaining pecan pie as Lionel read my typed pages.

"I know Harry Moran at the paper. He's an okay guy and owes me a favor. If I ask him to read your piece, I think he'd publish it. Like I said, it smacks of a Dicken's Christmas tale mixed with true crime drama. Should make for interesting reading by the public. Now that Marlon Powers is dead, he can't exactly sue you for defamation."

"Hmm, no he can't but his estate could. Do you think Margaret would object?"

"Ask her. You're going to have to tighten up the story before you submit it to Moran though. He sells advertising, remember. He can't sell the space you use by rambling on and on. Write up an article explaining the history and the facts and the sources corroborating those facts, like the mid-wife's diary and medical journal. That will carry some weight. I'd suggest you get it down to a thousand words or less," Lionel said.

"Good idea. I've got some work to do on the piece. Maybe if the truth is published by the newspaper, Silas Holt can finally find peace. I promised him I'd get to the bottom of this."

"Man, I don't even want to think of seeing that specter again."

Grannie chose that moment to materialize above Lionel and me in the office. *"Silas will be pleased. You've kept your promise. His soul can rest."*

"I hope so, Grannie. I'd hate to think of his angry ghost trapped at the inn and threatening me or my guests," I said.

*"Oh pooh, that's not likely to happen again. That storm was a once in a century blizzard that awakened him. You'll just have to trust me when I say we spirits behave ourselves,"* Grannie said with a chuckle that faded away as she vanished with a breath of cold air.

"Lord, I'll never get used to that woman popping in and out," Lionel whispered to me. His hand shook as he lifted his teacup.

# Chapter Nineteen

## Revenge

I had just laid out my finished article on the mahogany dining room table. A copy of the morning Gazette lay open next to the article. Harry Moran had published my article with front-page prominence. I wanted to compare the typed article I had submitted yesterday to the newspaper columns; it was all there, word for word. The editor hadn't changed one bit of it. The lamplight gleamed across the pages, every word heavy with the truth I'd uncovered: Silas Holt's innocence, Levi Powers' crime, and the cursed shadow their feud had cast for decades over Clarkstown.

Grannie's translucent light shone on the paper. *"You did good, baby girl. The whole town knows the truth now."*

I had meant for the article to bring peace ... to close the circle. But peace was the last thing in the air when the front door banged open. Moving into the foyer, I stared at the intruder.

Claire stood in the entrance, her face pale, eyes flashing with something dark. She held my article crumpled in her fist.

"You had no right," she hissed. "No right to print this. Do you know what you've done to Margaret? She read every word. The public will ridicule her. How can she face people? It nearly broke her."

I turned slowly, keeping my voice calm. "Claire, the truth is never easy ... but it's what this town has buried for over a century. The Powers family has gripped this town in its claws too long. Silas Holt didn't deserve what happened to him. And Marlon—"

"Stop!" she snapped, stepping forward. "You think you know the story, you're so smart. But you're missing the most important part ... my part!"

Her words chilled me more than the draft seeping in from the door. "Your part? What do you mean?"

I studied her face. My mind seeing the tortured face in the mirror, filled with rage before she masked it. This wasn't the timid girl she had pretended to be.

Claire's eyes flashed with fire. "I know who I am, Maddie. I've always known. Only pretended to come here as a naïve girl, fumbling for answers. I did my research long before I set foot in this inn and this town. I checked census records ... dug through archives. Yes, Margaret Quinton is my mother. But she's also Abigail Smith Holt's blood. That's right. Margaret is a descendant of Abigail Smith's sister, Mary."

My heart pounded in my chest. The Holt connection ... real and breathing in front of me. "Claire..."

She cut me off, her voice rising. "You wrote about the Powers' curse. About Holt's revenge. But you got it wrong."

She paced the floor, wringing her hands, back and forth between the front door and the parlor entrance. With every step, her anger built.

"I wanted my mother and real father to be a family, with me, like it should have been from the beginning. Marlon ruined it. He had to go. It wasn't supposed to end like this."

The room seemed to shrink around us as she told it.

"Tell me what I got wrong. Tell me what happened." I tried to coax her in a soft, calming voice, buying time for help to arrive ... Tom or Sally, anybody.

"I saw them," she said, her voice dropping to almost a whisper. "From my room, I was watching the snowflakes fall outside my bedroom window. Two men rode in on horseback, just as the storm began. They went into the barn. Curious, I slipped outside, hidden by the dark. I heard their argument ... saw John Kelce punch Marlon and leave him unconscious on the floor."

"John Kelce was here at the inn? How did you know him?" I asked, caught up in her story despite the danger radiating off her.

"John is my real father. I found his name on the birth records but that was the first time I ever saw him." Claire paced the narrow space. Her eyes darted about the room as if she expected someone to leap into sight. Her voice trembled with pent up emotion as she continued.

"I knew who Marlon was ... I'd seen him in town when I inquired about Margaret and heard him threaten to fix her little problem. It didn't take a genius to know I was the *little problem* he needed to fix."

"You told Sally you wanted to meet your birth mother. Was that a lie? Did you only pretend to be shy to win Sally's friendship? She cares for you. I think you planned on confronting Marlon not Margaret all along. Am I right?" I asked.

Her hand shook, but she lifted her chin, eyes locking onto mine with defiance. She shook her head vigorously, denying my claims.

From the corner of my eye, I spotted Grannie hovering above, watching the drama unfold. *"Be careful Maddie!"*

"Entering the barn, I faced John Kelce as he stood there staring down at Marlon Powers. I knew the truth about him long before you and Allen pieced it together." She laughed a harsh laugh and advanced toward me.

I stepped backward, keeping space between us.

"Kelce just stood there stupidly with a funny look on his face when I told him who I was and that he was my father. Do you know what he said?" Her voice cracked. "He denied me. Said he was just a kid when he and Margaret were together. That I wasn't his responsibility. He left me standing there as if I meant nothing. John Kelce just shook his head at me, said he was sorry, but it was too late in his life to become a father. He rode away, leaving me standing in that barn like a piece of trash!"

*"Careful Maddie. Claire appears to be ready to do something crazy,"* Grannie whispered as if anyone else but me could hear her.

I swallowed hard; the silence pressed down like the storm outside that night. Inching toward the kitchen, my eyes focused on the cell phone resting on the counter. I had to call for help. Claire's anger was building, and her grip on reality slipped with each word she spoke.

Claire's breath hitched. "And there was Marlon Powers ... sprawled drunk, pathetic ... the man who ruined my mother's life. Who planned to hurt me, too. He was going to fix the problem, well I decided to fix him first! All that rage ... it just boiled over; guess I couldn't help myself. I grabbed the lantern and hit him. Again and again until he didn't move and then I dropped it into the snow. Funny, you know, I watched the lamp oil spill out into the snow, like blood oozing from a body." She stared out the window into the distance as if seeing the scene in her mind.

"Did you put the rope around Marlon's neck? How did Marlon get into the tree, Claire? Did you do that?" I asked.

"What? No!" she whispered, her voice breaking. "I saw it. Him ... Silas Holt. His ghost. The same as he looked later on Christmas Eve. He was there, Maddie. The ghost saw Powers' body in the barn. Suddenly, Marlon's body floated upward like a puppet on a string and Silas hung him in that burned tree ... just like they did to him. He took his revenge. I was afraid he'd come for me next."

The image of Marlon Powers swinging from the elm tree had

been seared into my brain when I first saw him and now Claire's words brought it all back in vivid horrific detail.

"What did you do when Silas levitated the body?"

"Ran. I ran back to the front of the house, sneaked inside, and got to my room while you were all talking in the kitchen. The parlor was empty. When you and Sally checked on me later, I told you I was sick. You believed me. But I was scared and wet from plunging into the deep snow. I was afraid to come out."

Her confession hung in the air, thick and poisonous. My pulse roared in my ears.

She buried her face in her hands; her shoulders shook in raw emotion, exhausting her.

I stood frozen, the weight of her words pressing down. The truth of Silas Holt ... the truth of Marlon Powers ... the truth of Claire herself. My article was only half the story. The rest— the darker, more terrible half— had just spilled out like oil from the shattered lantern.

The silence in the house was unbearable after Claire's confession. Her sobs had quieted to shallow breaths, but the weight of her words pressed into me like the chill of grave dirt. Moving toward the kitchen, I inched backward, easing the swinging door open. Reaching for my cell phone to call for help, I paused when the crunch of boots on the porch reached my ears. Claire jerked her head up, hearing the same noise. Suddenly alert, she looked like a wounded animal.

The front door swung open, and in rushed Allen and Lucas, their eyes immediately locked onto the scene before them. The newspaper lay crumpled on the floor. Claire, pale and wild-eyed, sprung upward and shook her fist at the advancing men.

"Stay back!" Claire shouted in a strident voice.

"Claire," Allen started, his voice calm but edged, "we need to talk about your meeting in the barn with John Kelce and Marlon Powers. Move away from Maddie now and we'll ..."

He didn't get the words out before Claire bolted into the kitchen, pushing me with her, fury flashing like lightning across her face.

"My father threw me away! Everyone abandoned me!" she screamed.

And before I could move, she lunged toward the kitchen counter, her hand closing around the gleaming handle of a sharp knife.

The blade caught the overhead light as she whirled and pressed it against my throat. The cold kiss of steel froze my breath.

"Stay back," she cried.

"Claire ..." Allen's voice cut sharp but low, steady as stone as he approached. His hand lifted, palm open. "You don't want to do this."

Her grip trembled, but her eyes locked on Allen. "He deserved to die. Don't you see? He hurt my family ... Abigail's family. He threatened to hurt me, but I fixed him. Margaret can live in peace now without him. We'll have a happy life ... my mother and me."

I swallowed hard, my pulse pounding so hard I thought the knife moved with each pulse. "Claire ... you're not alone. You have friends," I whispered. "Hurting me won't help Margaret or alter the history of Abigail's death."

"Shut up!" she snarled, jerking me backward toward the outside kitchen door. Each step was a tug, my heels scraping against the polished tile. Allen followed, slow and steady, his words soft as falling snow.

"You don't want her blood on your hands, Claire. That's not who you are. Let her go."

Her breathing grew ragged, her steps clumsy. And then ...

Claire's foot came down on a furry tail.

Prissy shrieked, the most god-awful caterwaul I'd ever heard, and shot across the floor like a streak of lightning. Claire startled; the knife wobbled just an inch. Instinct took over. I drove my elbow hard into her ribs. She gasped, bending over, her grip loosened, and in that split second Allen surged forward.

His hand clamped onto her wrist, twisting sharply until the knife clattered to the floor. Lucas was there in an instant, grabbing her free arm. Claire collapsed to her knees, sobbing as Allen wrenched the weapon away.

"It's over," Allen said firmly, cuffs snapping closed around her wrists. "We heard everything. Claire Jennings, you're under arrest for the murder of Marlon Powers."

The knife lay on the tiled floor, a shard of silver in the glow of forgotten holiday candles. My throat stung where the blade had pressed, but the greater ache was in my chest … grief, pity, and relief all tangled up like garland on a tree.

I clung to Allen as he wrapped me in his strong arms and held me against his chest.

"That was too close for comfort," he said.

Allen lifted his gaze to Lucas, their silent understanding hanging heavier than the winter clouds outside.

Allen finally spoke, quietly but resolute. "No one needs to know how Marlon's body ended up in that tree."

Lucas nodded, his hand steady on Claire's shoulder. "That secret stays buried."

Minutes later, Luke started barking and jumping up and down. The front door opened and closed. A familiar voice rang out, and my ears couldn't believe what I heard. I pulled out of Allen's embrace and dashed into the foyer. My father stood grinning at me while Luke spun in circles.

"Hello Maddie-girl! Merry Christmas! I'm sorry I couldn't get home sooner." He dropped his duffel bag onto the floor and greeted me with open arms. A hug never felt so warm and loving.

"Welcome home, Dad. I can't believe you're here. You've made my holiday complete." I hugged him tighter, not believing my eyes then finally pulled away. "Come into the kitchen and meet everyone," I said.

Holding his hand, I led him into the kitchen, where Lucas and Allen waited with Claire in handcuffs. Both men looked at the older man and laughed at his puzzled expression.

"This is my boyfriend, Detective Allen Crawford, and his partner, Detective Lucas Wampler. They were, uh, just leaving."

"What's going on around here? I assume this young woman is in custody?" David Brooke asked. He glanced between the two men and me.

"Yes, she is. It's a long story but we've got all night to tell it," I said.

# Chapter Twenty

## New Year's Eve

I could hardly believe the transformation of the Legion post. Someone had scrubbed the place from floor to ceiling. Usually it smelled faintly of fried chicken dinners and pipe smoke, but tonight it shimmered with strings of white lights, tables laden with sparkling silver centerpieces on black linen tablecloths, glowing candles, and the low hum of a four-piece band warming up. The air carried the mingled pleasant scents of roasted meats, sugared pecans, and perfume from half the women in Clarkstown.

My sapphire blue gown caught the light each time I moved, its silk cool against my skin and bare neck where I had swept my blonde hair up into a French twist. I tugged self-consciously at the low neckline until Allen caught my hand and whispered, "You look like you stepped straight out of a dream." His tuxedo, crisp and black, fit him like a second skin, but it was his eyes ... steady, warm, intent ... that made me flush.

Across the room, Lily dazzled in a deep red dress with a beaded bodice that caught the light like frosted holly berries. Her long black hair draped her shoulders, the sides caught up in sequined clasps.

Lucas stayed close by her side, his hand never straying far from hers. Their laughter rose above the buzz of conversation.

And then there was Lionel ... dear Lionel ... strutting about in his white tux jacket, rose-colored cummerbund and bow tie, looking like a peacock among sparrows. He'd already gathered a little orbit of attention, mostly handsome veterans who seemed delighted by his sharp wit and shameless flirting.

My father reluctantly joined us for the New Year's Eve party only because I insisted he had to since he missed Christmas. He donned a dark navy blue suit and looked very handsome in my eyes. I watched him approach the buffet, filling a plate piled high with deviled eggs and ham biscuits, shaking his head at Lionel's antics. When he stepped up to the bar and joked with the bartender, I knew he felt at ease.

The gang was all here. Our turn to howl and celebrate the new year and the conclusion of our ghastly Christmas mystery. Delivering our delayed Christmas presents, we all cheered and made a big fuss over each gift. Lucas gifted Lily with a lovely pendant necklace, and Lionel received his favorite color, pink, turtleneck from me.

"I love it! Simply love it. I'll wear it tomorrow," exclaimed Lionel.

I gave Allen a book of Southern Appalachian history that I hoped he would enjoy, and he surprised me with a bottle of perfume and a silk scarf.

"Is that your fragrance? You won't believe how many perfume counters I visited, smelling one bottle after another until I found the one that reminded me of you," Allen said.

"Oh, that's so sweet. It's perfect, just like you," I said and kissed him on the cheek.

Lily gave Lucas a handmade knit sweater in his school colors.

"How did you know?" Lucas asked. "My former school sweater shrunk to about a size two recently. It got mixed up in a load of laundry and thrown into the dryer."

My father surprised me by bringing home a Christmas gift he bought in Hong Kong ... a scarlet silk kimono with an intricate lotus blossom pattern woven into the fabric.

"If you don't wear that, I'd love to borrow it," Lily said with a chuckle. "I can think of the perfect occasion," she said with a wink to Lucas.

We all filled our plates from the buffet, laughing and enjoying each other's company. Good food, fine wine, and loving friends to end the holiday season and welcome in the start of a new year. New beginnings.

Music filled the main hall, warm brass and lilting strings as couples drifted to the dance floor. Allen offered his hand to me with a small bow. "May I?"

I smiled, letting him lead me. His hand was firm at the small of my back, his steps sure as we moved in time with the music. The world narrowed to his closeness, his breath warm against my temple, the faint scent of cedar and cologne mixing with the champagne that lingered on my tongue.

"For once," I said softly, "it feels like we can just enjoy the moment. No ghosts, no killers, no storms."

"Don't jinx it, Maddie," he murmured, though his grin told me he agreed.

When the countdown began, the entire room seemed to hold its breath. Ten ... nine ... the band swelled and voices joined in, glasses lifted. Allen's hand tightened in mine. Two, one ... Happy New Year!

Confetti rained down, champagne corks popped, and Allen kissed me. Not the careful peck of caution, but a passionate kiss ... full, certain, and brimming with the promise of something more. The surrounding applause faded as I melted into his arms, letting myself believe that maybe, just maybe, the year ahead would be brighter.

Later, when the last dance had ended and the final toast had been made, Allen drove me and my dad back to Magnolia Blossom. The snow sparkled in the moonlight, crisp and undisturbed, while the inn stood proud and welcoming after its long siege of secrets.

Inside, Grannie was waiting, her form shimmering in the lamplight. She gave me a knowing look, then beckoned me silently toward the back door. I followed. Allen lingered, but I grabbed his hand and pulled him along with me. My father followed us, with a curious look on his face.

"Why are you going outside, Maddie?" David asked.

The night was hushed, the only sound being the tapping of my high heels on the porch. And then I saw them.

Silas Holt stood beneath the lightning-struck tree, his posture tall but no longer burdened with rage. At his side was a woman, her face kind, her hand looped through his arm ... Abigail. Her spirit glowed as luminous as candlelight, but the love between them was brighter than any lantern.

They gazed at one another, then toward us. Silas raised his hand in a slow wave, his eyes meeting mine, then Grannie's. Gratitude, peace, release ... it was all there in that one simple gesture.

Grannie's voice whispered at my side. *Justice has been told, Maddie. The truth has set them free.*

I blinked, and in that breath, they were gone. Only the swaying branches of the broken elm remained, somber and still.

The cold air prickled my cheeks, but warmth spread in my chest. The curse of the Powers' name, the tragedy of Holt ... it had all finally come full circle.

Allen wrapped his arms around me.

"Did I really see that? Tell me it wasn't a dream," Allen whispered.

"You saw it. Love that has united two people throughout time. Wasn't it beautiful?"

"What did you two just see? I think I've been away too long; strange things are happening here."

Grannie materialized in front of her son. I heard him gasp right before his knees buckled, and he promptly collapsed onto the porch floor.

*"Leave them alone right now, son. They need some privacy. We've got a lot of catching up to do,"* Grannie spoke in a whisper.

I shot her a nod toward my dumbfounded father and laughed into the dark night.

We stepped back inside. Allen gathered me to him and kissed me long and lovingly.

And I knew ... this New Year had begun not only with endings but with the promise of new beginnings too.

# Acknowledgments

Thank you Pamela Earley and David M. Romano for their ***Pamela Bella's Southern Style Cookbook*** and for sharing her delicious recipes for Clam Chowder and Fried Oysters, a traditional Appalachian holiday meal that is enjoyed by the guests of the Magnolia Blossom Inn at Christmas. Also, Christmas wouldn't be complete without a traditional Southern Pecan Pie as described in this marvelous cookbook.

# Recipes

## Fried Oysters

***Fried Oysters***

**Ingredients:**

2 eggs
1/4 teaspoon of salt
1/4 cup of milk
1/2 cup of flour
2 pints of fresh shucked oysters
1 cup of self-rising cornmeal

**Preparation:**

Combine eggs, milk, flour, and salt in a mixing bowl and stir until smooth. Dip oysters in batter. Roll in cornmeal.

Fry in pan with bacon grease until golden brown.

*Pamela Bella's Southern Style Cookbook, page 24

# Recipes

## Clam Chowder

***Clam Chowder***

**Ingredients:**

2 quarts of shucked clams

2 cups half & half cream

3 slices of cooked, chopped bacon

4 large potatoes and 1 large onion

1 teaspoon salt and 1/2 teaspoon pepper

1 stick of butter (1/2 cup)

**Preparation:**

Cube potatoes and cook till tender in a large pot. Drain.

Add diced onions and butter into mixture.

Add clams, half & half cream, salt and pepper in pot.

Add chopped bacon.

Simmer for 30 minutes.

* This is a Vermont-style clam chowder with a Southern twist. Pamela Bella's Southern Style Cookbook on page 44.

# Recipes
## Southern Pecan Pie


***Southern Pecan Pie***
### Ingredients:
1 teaspoon of butter and 1 cup of sugar

1 teaspoon vanilla and 1 cup chopped pecans

3 eggs, slightly beaten and 1 cup dark corn syrup

1 pastry shell unbaked- 9 inch

1/2 cup of pecan halves for topping

### Preparation:
Cream butter and sugar together.

Add eggs, dark corn syrup, vanilla and chopped pecans.

Mix well in bowl then pour into pastry shell

Arrange decorative pecan halves on top of pie.

Place on lower oven shelf to bake at 300 degrees Fahrenheit
for 45 minutes or until center is firm.


Pamela Bella's Southern Style Cookbook on pages 33-34.

# Author Biography

An avid reader since childhood, **Nancy M. Wade** always enjoyed writing stories and upon formal retirement in 2012, she decided to pursue her passion. Nancy has written five historical novels, including a western action adventure trilogy called the *"Circle-D Saga"*. A lover of all things mysterious, Nancy created two cozy mystery series. *"A Meadowood Mystery"* is set in a small Ohioan town with amateur sleuth and housewife, Meredith Gardner. There are eight novels to date in this series. The *"Maddie Brooke Mystery"* series includes four cozy paranormal novels centered in a historic, southern bed-and-breakfast inn where recent college graduate turned sleuth, Maddie Brooke, resides with her German shepherd, Luke, and her grandmother's spirited ghost.

Nancy is a member of the Tri-Cities Lost State Writers Guild and is an honors graduate of East Tennessee State University. You can follow her author pages on Instagram and Facebook or her web site at: https://nancymwadeauthor.com.